KILL OR BE KILLED

I drew two beads from Marines on the roof of a three-story bank. I ran at them, launched into a *gozt*, and blasted the first woman off her perch. She tumbled to the ground, rebounding several times before her skin faded. In the meantime, the second woman spun and leveled her rifle on me as I rose and started for her.

"I don't have to kill you," she said.

"That's your job."

"Don't come any closer."

I did.

She fired.

The bead struck my skin, rebounded, and I was on her, knocking the rifle from her grip and withdrawing my Ka-Bar.

"You should have killed me," I said, then closed my eyes and punched her with the blade . . .

Also by Ben Weaver

BROTHERS IN ARMS

REBELS IN ARMS

BEN WEAVER

An Imprint of HarperCollinsPublishers

For Kendall and Lauren
Who remind me that we are all children . . .

This is a work of fiction. Names, characters, places, and incidents are products of the author's imagination or are used fictitiously and are not to be construed as real. Any resemblance to actual events, locales, organizations, or persons, living or dead, is entirely coincidental.

EOS
An Imprint of HarperCollins*Publishers*
10 East 53rd Street
New York, New York 10022-5299

Copyright © 2002 by Ben Weaver
Excerpt from *Hammerfall* copyright © 2001 by C. J. Cherryh
Excerpt from *Rebels in Arms* copyright © 2002 by Ben Weaver
Excerpt from *Trapped* copyright © 2002 by James Alan Gardner
Excerpt from *Acorna's Search* copyright © 2001 by Hollywood.Com, Inc.
Excerpt from *The Mystic Rose* copyright © 2001 by Stephen R. Lawhead
ISBN: 0-06-000625-0
www.eosbooks.com

First Eos paperback printing: September 2002

Eos Trademark Reg. U.S. Pat. Off. And in Other Countries, Marca Registrada, Hecho en U.S.A.
HarperCollins® is a trademark of Harper Collins Publishers Inc.

Printed in the U.S.A

10 9 8 7 6 5 4 3 2 1

Acknowledgments

I'm indebted to Jennifer Brehl and Diana Gill at Eos for their support and encouragement. Without them, Captain Scott St. Andrew would have seen early retirement at the end of book one!

My agent, John Talbot, continues to inspire me with his keen wit and pragmatic advice regarding the publishing industry.

Finally, both Robert Drake and Caitlin Blasdell helped me create this series, and I know they're very proud of what we've accomplished.

The Seventeen System Guard Corps
Articles of the Code of Conduct
Revised 2301
(adopted from old United States Marine Corps Articles)

ARTICLE I

I will always remember that I am a Colonial citizen, fighting in the forces that preserve my world and our way of life. I have resigned to give my life in their defense.

ARTICLE II

I will never surrender of my own volition. If in command, I will never surrender the members of my command while they still have the will and/or the means to resist.

ARTICLE III

If I am captured, I will continue to resist by any and all means available. I will make every effort to escape and to aid others to escape. I will accept neither parole nor special favors from the enemy.

ARTICLE IV

If I become a prisoner of war, I will keep faith with my fellow prisoners. I will give no information nor take part in any action which might be harmful to fellow Colonial citizens. If I am senior, I will take command. If not, I will obey the lawful orders of those appointed over me and will uphold them in every way.

ARTICLE V

Should I become a prisoner of war, I am required to give name, rank, and willingly submit to retinal and DNA analysis. I will evade answering further questions to the utmost of my ability and will not consciously submit to cerebral scans of any kind. I will make no oral, written, or electronic statements disloyal to the colonies or harmful to their cause.

ARTICLE VI

I will never forget that I am fighting for freedom, that I am responsible for my actions, and that I am dedicated to the principles that make my world free. I will trust in my god or gods and in the Colonial Alliance forever.

PART 1

◄ ►

Campaign Exeter

From my seat on the dais, I looked over the crowd of cadets about to graduate from South Point Academy. Could they really listen to a middle-aged soldier like me drone on about the challenges of being an officer? After all, the commandant, a war vet himself, was already at the lectern and boring them to death with that speech. In fact, when the commandant had asked me to speak, I had panicked because I knew those kids needed something more than elevated diction and fancy turns of phrase. But what?

The commandant glanced over his shoulder and nodded at me. "And now ladies and gentlemen, at this time I'd like to introduce a man whose Special Ops Tactical Manual is required reading here at the academy, a man whose treatise on Racinian conditioning transformed that entire program. Ladies and gentlemen, I give you Colonel Scott St. Andrew, chief of the Alliance Security Council."

Applause I had expected, but a standing ovation? Or maybe those cadets were just overjoyed that the commandant was leaving the podium. I dragged myself up, wincing over all the metal surgeons had jammed into me after the nanotech regeneration had failed. Unless you were really looking for it, you wouldn't notice my limp. I tugged at the hems of my dress tunic, raised my shoulders, and took a deep breath before starting forward. The kids continued with their applause, their eyes wide and brimming with naïveté.

"Thank you. Please . . ." I gestured for them to sit, then waited for the rumble to subside. "First, let me extend my gratitude to the commandant for allowing me to be here today." I tipped my head toward the man, who winked. "As all of you know, we are living in some very turbulent times. The treaties we signed at the end of the war are now being violated. Rumors of yet another civil war persist. But let me assure you that we at the security council are doing everything we can to resolve these conflicts. Now then. I didn't come here to talk about current events. I came here to tell you what you want to hear—a war story—not because it's entertaining, but because it's something you need to hear . . ."

I lay in my quarters aboard the SSGC *Auspex*, cushioned tightly in my gelrack and in the middle of a disturbing dream. My name wasn't Scott St. Andrew; I wasn't an eighteen-year-old captain and company commander in the Seventeen System Guard Corps, in charge of one hundred and sixty-two lives; and my cheek no longer bore the cross-shaped birthmark that revealed I had a genetic defect and came from poor colonial stock.

In the dream I was a real Terran, born in New York, and about to download my entire college education through a cerebro. I sat in a classroom with about fifty other privileged young people who would never need to join the military as a way to escape from their stratified society. I looked down at the C-shaped device sitting on the desk in front of me. I need only slide it onto my head and learn.

But I couldn't. I was afraid I might forget who I was, forget that my father, an overworked, underpaid company geologist, had tried his best to raise me and my brother Jarrett, since my mother had left us when we were small. Jarrett and I had entered South Point Academy just when the war had begun, and Jarrett had died in an accident during a "conditioning process" developed by an ancient alien race we called the Racinians. The conditioning, which involved the introduction into our brains of mnemosyne—a species of eidetic parasite found aboard Racinian spacecraft—enhanced our physical and mental capabilities . . . *and* aged us at an accelerated rate.

No, I couldn't forget. I needed to remember what I had become, because I sensed even then that if just one person could learn something from my story, from my mistakes, then the universe might forgive me my sins.

They were many.

So I sat there, watching the others put on their cerebroes and flinch as the datalock took hold. Some grinned as they were "enlightened." All that cerebroed data became a part of them, while I would rather my life, all that I had done, become a part of it. Still, I wonder if anyone will really care about the war between the alliances and the seventeen colonial systems a thousand years from now. Future generations might never understand that in the year 2301, hundreds of thousands died in the name of what United States president Abraham Lincoln had once called "a just and lasting peace." They died for a cause, and for those untouched by war, that is too often incomprehensible. I knew that even the young people in that room had no true concept of war. I wished I could teach them, but all I could do was sit there until the shipboard alarm yanked me out of the dream.

I sprang from my rack, expecting the captain's voice to boom over the shipwide comm. Nothing. The alarm droned on and drove me to the hatchcomm. I dialed up Lieutenant Colonel Jeffery Disque, Twenty-second Battalion Commander, a middle-aged man with buttery brown skin and a striking shock of gray at just one temple. He eyed me with disgust, then spoke in a voice hoarse from screaming at insubordinates. "What is it, Captain?"

"Sorry, sir. Thought maybe you knew why the Klaxon sounded."

Disque yawned, his lip beginning to quiver. There I was, some antsy kid who had beeped him out of slumber. The first time I had met him, I had an immediate sense of just how ill proportioned his ego had become. You could fit planets, star systems, entire nebulae inside the thing. Then again, having a battalion commander who thought he could live forever wasn't always a bad thing, especially when the rounds were flying. He would never order another company to turn tail on yours, and you might even find him outside his command tent, pumping off rounds himself . . .

I cleared my throat, grew more tense as he just looked at me, failing to answer. "Do you know why the Klaxon sounded, sir?"

He screwed his sour puss into a tighter knot. "'Course I know why that goddamned alarm is going. You think I'm a brainwipe, Captain?"

"Sir, no, sir."

"That's a nav alarm. We're changing course."

"Sir?"

"We just got new orders, Captain."

"We're not going to Kennedy-Centauri?"

"Nope."

"Then who is? Those people in Plymouth Colony need us. You saw the holos. Civvies are getting shot in the streets."

"Then whoever's left better hide, 'cause the Twenty-second Battalion ain't going there."

"We have to send somebody." Disque could not have known that my own life depended upon us reaching Kennedy-Centauri, not that he would have cared.

"Bandage your bleeding heart, Captain. I'm sure they'll dispatch another element. We got a more interesting op. I know you're going to like it. The briefing alert will hit your tablets in a couple of minutes."

"Aye-aye, sir."

"Anything else, Captain?"

"Uh, no, sir. Thank you, sir."

He flashed an ugly grin and nodded.

Even as I switched off the hatchcomm, it rang again. Someone was at my door: Rooslin Halitov. I let him in. He steered himself directly to the chair at my desk and sat, scratching nervously at his jaw.

A year prior, I would never have imagined that a cadet who had tried to take my life, a cadet who had despised me more than anyone else in his world, would eventually turn down his own shot at company commander to become my executive officer. One look at the guy—blocky jaw, blond hair, barrel chest, flaming blue eyes—made you think, yeah, he was the neighborhood bully. And Rooslin had grown up to become academy bully. Then, after we had both seen and had doled out more death than the Corps could have ever warned us about, we had become uneasy friends. His transformation had not come without a price.

"Know what that alarm's saying to me?" Halitov asked. "It's saying: you're fucked."

"We both are—'cause we're not going to Kennedy-Centauri."

"Shit . . ." He rubbed eyes full of sleep grit, eyes that had looked years younger only a few months prior. "You talk to Breckinridge?"

"Just found out myself." I crossed to my gelrack, dropped heavily onto the mattress. "She can't change this." I sighed out my frustration. "Anyway, Disque says we'll get the decrypted poop in about twenty minutes."

"Fuck Disque. I hate that prick. He's going to get us all killed, then stand on the big pile of bodies and give his victory speech: 'These young men and women have given their lives so that the seventeen systems might one day be freed from Alliance tyranny . . .' Yeah, they gave their lives so you'd have a soap box to stand on, you asshole."

"Next time we're out drinking, I'm going to pay you to do that. Of course the old man will show up behind you."

"This ain't funny . . ." His sober expression dampened my smile. Thankfully, the hatchcomm beeped again, distracting us from feeling any more sorry for ourselves. I checked the monitor. It was our Accelerated Assimilation Trainer, Captain Kristi Breckinridge, who, with short, dark hair gelled back and a body conditioned to machinelike precision, could steal some officers' breaths with a salacious glance or a chokehold, depending upon her mood or how obviously they had gawked at her. I opened the hatch.

"Captain," she said, then didn't wait for an invitation and pushed past me. "Shut the door." She regarded Halitov with a curt nod, turned her clandestine expression back on me. "He has to leave."

"He stays."

A dangerous realization lit her gaze. "You haven't told him, have you? You understand that information is highly classified . . ."

"Told me what?" said Halitov, feigning ignorance.

"Sit down, shut up," I said, then faced Breckinridge, trembling with the realization that I would stand up to her, be honest with her—even reveal that I had done some research on her past and discovered things that made me distrust her even more. If she wanted me to play her game, I'd play—but by my rules. "He knows everything. And you're going to help him, too."

She swore under her breath, closed her eyes. "Scott, that wasn't the deal. He hasn't been invited to become a Warden."

I looked at her, grew rigid. "You came in here, said the Colonial Wardens—the most powerful and elite group in the Seventeen System Guard Corps—wants to recruit me. Turns out you guys are running a little coup to motivate the new government and want me to help. Then you tell me you know something about my brother, get me thinking that maybe he's not dead, and finally, you promise me that I can meet a woman on Kennedy-Centauri who has epineuropathy just like me, only her conditioning process is perfect, and she's got three times the strength and endurance of the average conditioned soldier. You say you can fix me, make me like her, 'cause the Wardens have found a second conditioning facility on Aire Wu, when everyone thinks there's just one, on Exeter, currently occupied by Alliance troops. If I ever do get reconditioned, if there is a cure to this rapid aging, then I'm *not* going to keep that information classified. Every conditioned solider deserves to know about and receive that cure, and the first one in line is going to be him." I pointed at Halitov.

"You'll do what we tell you—or you'll get nothing," she snapped.

"I'm not sure I want anything from people like you. I know what happened at the academy, the hazing and the cheating—"

She snickered. "Don't you have better things to do than pry into my life?"

"Not when mine's on the line. They cleared you, but you were guilty, I bet. Then you graduate, try to get into the Wardens, but the request is denied five times—until the CO who's been denying the request suddenly changes his mind. I talked to an old buddy of yours, Grimwald. He told me just how you got that CO to change his mind."

Her cheeks flushed. "If I were you, I wouldn't say another word."

"But I'm not done. We haven't even gotten to your brother. Yeah, I know about him, too. Disabled and abandoned. Your parents are gone. He's all you have in the world. So why is he still there, rotting away in that hospital?"

She eyed me for a moment, then, in the next second, she reached out with her mind into the quantum bond between particles and crawled across the bulkhead behind me, shifting like some arachnid unimpeded by gravity. She slipped in and got me in her patented chokehold. Her voice came low and harsh, directly into my ear: "You . . . don't . . . know . . . anything."

"I know you're an opportunist. You have no honor, no loyalty."

"What I have . . . is your life in my hands."

Out of the corner of my eye, I saw Halitov jab a pistol into Breckinridge's head. "Let him go," he said.

She thought a moment, then ripped her arm away, shoved me aside. "You want to push my buttons? I can push yours. Should we talk about your mother?"

I massaged my neck, felt a sudden tightness in my chest.

"Oh, spare me this bullshit," groaned Halitov, his expression turning emphatic. "We're dying. We need to be reconditioned."

"That's right," I said, then glared at Breckinridge. "He gets reconditioned—or I don't even meet with your people—whenever that's going to happen, because we're no longer en route to Kennedy-Centauri."

"I knew that before the nav alarm sounded. We'll reschedule. I sent word to my people on a chip tawted out just five minutes ago."

"I hope this little meeting will be soon," said Halitov.

Breckinridge's stare turned menacing. "It will be." She took a deep breath, sighed heavily. "Got more news for you. We've done some studies on the aging side effects. In one month you might age a standard year. In the next month, you might age only three, four months, in the following month, you might age naturally. We haven't found a pattern or a way to predict the effects yet."

"Oh, that makes me feel all warm and tingly," sang Halitov. "Tomorrow I wake up, and my bones are cracking and my hair's falling out and I can't even remember that I had a sex drive, which, by that time, won't be driving me anywhere, anymore."

"Shut up," I told him, then gestured that Breckinridge go on.

"We have learned that as the aging progresses, there's a long-term memory imbalance that interferes with the short-term. You can't remember if you shut off the vid, and you can't stop reciting some obscure data cerebroed into the deepest parts of your mind."

"I've seen that effect," I said, recalling an old woman from the Minsalo Caves, a recently young old woman who had become a misfiring human computer, confused and ultimately suicidal.

"Finally, I do have some good news," Breckinridge said, brightening slightly.

Halitov rolled his eyes. "This I have to hear."

"I know where you're headed."

I raised my brows. "Really?"

Within an hour of our conversation with Breckinridge we were tawting out seventy-five light-years
from Earth to the moon Exeter. Halitov and I had met
there at South Point Academy, but our training to become officers had been interrupted by the war. I
never thought I'd return to the place where my career
had begun, but I later learned that Halitov and I were
shipped there because our friend Mary Brooks, chief
of the Colonial Security Council, had orchestrated
our transfer to the Exeter Campaign: #345EX7-B. We
would, she hoped, take back control of the academy
and the damaged conditioning facility from Alliance
occupation troops. She also knew we would satisfy
our curiosity regarding our friends Paul Beauregard
and Dina Anne Forrest. During a black Op, Dina had
been killed, and in love with her, Paul had gone
AWOL to take her to the Minsalo Caves on Exeter,
where he thought she might be revived because a
strange healing process occurred there, one I had experienced firsthand. The idea that a cave could raise
the dead seemed ludicrous, but there were alien arti-
facts within those caverns, and history is woven with
stories of places that heal the body and the soul.

Thus, Paul Beauregard, son of the famous Colonel
Beauregard, head of the Colonial Wardens, thought
he could save the woman he loved, and the last we
had heard, Alliance Marines had found his ship but
not him or Dina. More than ever, I hoped that he had
succeeded, and I already burned to abandon my

mission and head out to the caves to find out for my-self. My own heart ached for Dina, though some-where deep inside I had already begun to accept her death.

We reached the Jovian-like gas giant of 70 Virginis b, and Halitov and I took in the view through a nar-row porthole.

"Weird coming back, huh?" he asked.

"Yeah."

"You think Beauregard really got her into the caves?"

"Who knows."

He nudged my shoulder. "Hey, that was some smooth negotiating with Breckinridge. I really liked the part where you brought up her disabled brother. *Real* smooth."

I gave him a dirty look. "She's scum."

"No, she's hot."

"If you had a disabled brother, wouldn't you want to be there for him, care for him? Would you leave him to rot away with strangers?"

"I don't know . . ."

"Well, I do."

We stayed there for a few minutes, neither saying a word until the order to drop came in.

The insertion went off well, with the loss of only one troop ship. Within an hour we stood outside my com-mand tent, watching artillery fire stitch across the night sky above the academy. Relentless enemy gun-ners played connect the dots with the constellations, or so it appeared.

In the valley below, our three platoons stealthily

advanced toward the admin building, that great as-
semblage of isosceles triangles glowing in the tracer
light and framed by the distant mesas.

"I don't get it. We blanketed this place with EMP
bombs," said Halitov.

"Which knocked out all localized weaponry and
electronics," I said. "They've obviously resupplied.
Pulse wave's a singular event. Doesn't affect new
weapons brought into the area."

"Then I want to know how they rearmed themselves so quickly . . ."

"They must be making drops on the other side of
the moon, maybe out where Beauregard took us when
we stole that shuttle the last time we were here."

"Then how come our eyes in the sky haven't
picked up those crab carriers making drops?"

"I don't know."

"I say they got a cache already here, maybe under-
ground. Maybe out in the Minsalo Caves."

"Maybe—"

A tremendous boom just meters away cut off my
thought. From the corner of my eye, I saw that my
command tent had exploded in an upheaval of sparks
and sharp-edged debris.

"Son of a bitch!" cried Halitov.

Even as the shrapnel rained down, he and I
dropped to our bellies, reached for our wrists, and
tapped buttons on our tacs, activating our combat
skins. The phosphorescent membranes of energy en-
veloped us, and the Heads Up Viewers rippled to life,
superimposing themselves at an arm's length from
our faces and giving us reports of our own vital signs
and skin status, as well as troop movements and a half

dozen other options visible only to us. Once skinned, you could always tell when someone else's life force was drained just by examining how brightly they glowed in the standard green night-vision setting.

As usual Halitov wasn't glowing very brightly, not because his life force was drained but because the mere act of skinning always triggered his claustrophobia, and that fear, born of a childhood trauma in which he had been locked in a box for days by neighborhood bullies, took a heavy toll.

"Rooslin! You're okay, man! You're okay!" I shouted over our command frequency.

His reply resonated in the combat skin shimmering over my ears. "Yeah, yeah, but look at Javelin's platoon. He's only got one squad holding back. Javelin? Report!"

Before the second lieutenant could reply, I ordered my skin's computer to bring up a digitized image of Mr. James Javelin and his people as they advanced toward the administration building. But the three squads in his platoon weren't supposed to be advancing; they were supposed to remain on the perimeter and sweep for snipers or take out any bunkers containing artillery troops who might aim their big guns at mobile command bases—like my own—set up in the foothills. All right, Javelin had left one squad back, but those raw recruits were pinned down by fire from not only the administration building, but also from a rear attack by Alliance Marines positioned on the barracks' rooftops. I watched one recruit get his head blown off, followed by a second, who aimed his QQ90 particle rifle at some distant muzzle flash that became all too bright as he took a scintillating, accelerated round to the right eye. His head whipped back, and down he went—a man whose life I was responsible for, a man who had died because I had failed to recognize that one of my platoon leaders was not obeying orders, dammit.

The second lieutenant's tinny voice finally broke over the channel. "The Fourteenth and the Fifteenth have breached the admin building, Captain."

"All three of your squads were supposed to fall back," screamed Halitov.

"In theory, yeah, Captain. But you ain't down here looking at this defensive fire. The Fifty-first Platoon needed our help making the breach. And I didn't have no time to call back and wait for your okay. I gave it to them. If you got a problem with that, you come down and have a look for yourself—*sir*."

Halitov's reply came heated and fast over my private channel. "I'm payin' that motherfucker a visit."

"Wait—"

He charged off, his combat skin swarming with dark blotches as he switched the setting to camouflage. I watched him wind a tortuous path down the foothills for a few seconds, then vanish.

I lay there on my gut, monitoring the blips in my HUV, each representing one of my combatants. I zoomed in our now-popular second lieutenant, saw an image of him piped down from one of our satellites. He crouched behind a stone knee wall abutting one of the walkways. "Javelin? Copy?" I called.

"Yes, sir?"

"The XO's on his way. Before he gets there, I want you to pull your people out of admin and resume your supporting positions."

"I do that, sir, and we'll lose the Fifty-first."

"You don't know that. Pull your people out. That's a direct order."

"Communication terminated," said my onboard computer.

The bastard had cut the link.

My job as company commander, though sometimes complex, was pretty damned simple at the moment: monitor the actions of my three platoons to ensure that our objective of seizing the administration building was achieved. I was supposed to direct troops as needed and react accordingly to the defenses we encountered. I was not supposed to go down there and fight myself—

Which is exactly what I did.

As I charged down the hill, switching my skin to camouflage and feeling that familiar surge of adrenaline, one memory flashed repeatedly, as though locked inside a shard of tumbling glass. I saw my old instructor, Major Yokito Yakata, standing in our classroom and telling us about our newly conditioned bodies: *"Other forces of nature—the strong and weak nuclear forces, gravity, electromagnetism—we're all of these, and we're only beginning to discover the potential power here. One day, we'll abandon our TAWT drives and will ourselves across the galaxy."*

Willing myself to another location was something I had tried successfully already, but only for short distances, and the feat had left me weak and dazed. I had no desire to appear instantly at Javelin's side but be so spent by the journey that I could not effectively reprimand him.

Consequently, I was a ripe target as I raced across

the open field between the foothills and the admin building, reaching out into the quantum bond, believing I could accelerate my pace. But, as had frequently happened in the past, I didn't feel a damned thing.

A large formation of boulders adorned with plaques commemorating some of South Point's most prestigious graduates stood about twenty meters ahead—my only cover.

With particle fire digging ragged trenches within a meter or two of my path, I made the "difficult" decision to get the hell out of there. Even as I hauled ass, my computer issued the warning: "Particle fire locked on." In my HUV, a representation of my body appeared in a data bar, my skin glowing red in a region near my shoulder. I cocked my head, and yes, a stream of fire split the air, coming right at me. If that Marine held his bead for a little longer, it would eventually wear down and penetrate my skin.

"Come on, you son of a bitch," I muttered to myself, then leapt forward, reached out, found the bond between me, the air, the ground, and the boulders ahead.

Gozt is the bullet thrust, one of the quitunutul fighting arts that, in low G, turns you into a deadly projectile. At that moment, though, I was more interested in presenting the smallest possible target to the Marine behind me, and with me in the *gozt*, all he looked at was a pair of boots dematerializing into the night.

I reached the boulders, then broke forward out of the move, letting myself tumble once before landing hard, way too hard, on my feet. I staggered as the impact reverberated up my legs. Sensing the bond as a viscous gel I could mold, I prepared to dart from my cover, toward a pair of rear doors set within an alcove where I knew Javelin had positioned himself. More particle fire began chewing into the boulders, blasting away slabs of stone that sent me scurrying sideways, toward a deeper crevice near my knees.

The Marine who had first targeted me was now closing the gap. Knowing he had me pinned down, he would leap over the boulder and rack up his point-blank kill at any second.

I had to move. Looked to the rear doors. Saw a gauntlet of fire crisscrossing the way. Then, behind me, the firing suddenly stopped. I edged around the boulder, stole a look across the field. Nothing.

A pebble struck my shoulder. I looked up.

The Marine issued a hysterical cry as he dropped down from the rock, his skin fluctuating between green, black, and ocher.

My own particle rifle had been disintegrated in my tent, but I still had my blades, a pair of old-fashioned Ka-Bars kept in sheaths stitched onto my boots. I reached for them—

But he was on me, knocking me back with his boot and jabbing the muzzle of his particle rifle into my neck. Our skins crackled with reflected energy, though he had his setting low enough so that he wouldn't rebound violently.

Particle fire belched from his weapon, and a harsh, white light suddenly grew from the skin protecting my neck.

I caught a glimpse of the Marine's face. He was a kid like me, maybe eighteen, nineteen, so scared that he had whipped himself into a frenzy to get the job done. He wanted no guilt, no fear; he was merely neutralizing an enemy troop. Nothing personal.

His boot pressed harder. I reached up, tried to grab his leg, but all that reflected fire kicked my hands back. I probed for the bond. Gone again.

And that's when the fear, the real, unadulterated fear that wrenches you from a nightmare and keeps you up into the wee hours staring at the shadows, pinned me more effectively than the Marine ever could. I just lay there, watching the Reaper wave.

2 **Over twenty years** have passed since the night I was lying behind that boulder. I remember that moment as though it had happened only seconds ago. In fact, I can remember each and every soldier who has tried to take my life and every one whose life I have taken. This is the curse of having a memory so keen, so enhanced by alien technology that it is impossible to forget. And I wish I could forget how someone, I'm not sure who, perhaps myself, shouted in my ear, "Get up!" Those words, that feeling of urgency, penetrated the fear. I rolled out of that Marine's bead. He continued tracking me with his fire.

I shivered with relief as the bond returned, shy though it had been, and the Marine's water-slow movements confirmed that. As I came out of the roll, I reached up, seized the barrel of his rifle, and hauled myself up with it, despite his firing.

Shards of rock torn free by his rounds tumbled around us. Artillery continued booming overhead, along with the smaller arms fire slicing up the field around us, and it was difficult to hear him scream as I ripped the rifle out of his grip, then reached for his wrist, locking my grip around his tac. With fingers strengthened by the bond, I tore off the tac, taking his hand with it. His combat skin trickled away, dissolving down to his ankles as he clutched his ragged stump, his mouth working to form something that wouldn't come out. He spotted his severed appendage lying on the ground. "My hand," he finally cried. "My hand."

I had about three or four breaths to make a decision. I could kill him or just let him go. He seemed too shocked to pose a threat. I thought back to the last time I had been to Exeter and been faced with an identical situation. My decision then? The wrong one.

"It's okay," I told the Marine. "Just be quiet. It's okay." I shifted up to him, slid my arm around his back as I lifted my leg, fishing out my Ka-Bar. "It won't hurt anymore."

For a second, he looked down, saw my Ka-Bar coming toward his gray-and-azure utilities, and said, "Tell my mom I'm sorry . . ."

Before he finished, I buried the knife in his heart. He looked at me, eyes going vague as he slumped in my arms. I let him fall, shuddered, withdrew my knife. Stood there. Swallowed.

I had just robbed a mother of her son. I hated myself as the tug and pull of war made me shudder once more. I hated myself, but I refused to become a victim of my own guilt. Sergeant Judiah Pope, my old squad leader, had been killed by a Marine whom I had shown mercy. So I killed that Marine behind the boulder with extreme prejudice, and there are those who still hate me for this, call my actions brutal and unnecessary. They were brutal. Unnecessary? It was war.

I took off and found Javelin, a husky kid with dark, curly hair and the face of an angry St. Bernard, along with his platoon sergeant, a lanky blond woman named Fanjeaux. They huddled in the alcove, their gazes far away as they monitored images in their HUVs.

"Lieutenant Javelin," I barked as I scrambled into the alcove. Then it dawned on me. Only two of them were there. "Where's Captain Halitov?"

It took a moment for Javelin to pry himself from his screens. "Sir?"

"Where's Captain Halitov?"

"Sir, I don't know, sir. And with all due respect, I'm busy right now." His gaze went distant. "Tao, Rumi, Jackson? Fall back to that second corridor. Now!"

"Hey, Mandella, Rickover? What're you doing?" asked Fanjeaux incredulously. "Move out!"

I activated my HUV, ordered the computer to show me Halitov's location.

"Unable to locate Captain Halitov."

"What do you mean?"

The computer repeated stoically, "Unable to locate Captain Halitov."

"Has his tac been removed?"

"Unknown."

I opened the command channel. "Rooslin? Copy?"

Particle fire drummed along the wall behind us.

"Captain? We have to move," cried Javelin.

"Rooslin? Do you copy?"

If he did, I couldn't tell.

A standard artillery shell whirred in, dropping no more than ten meters beside us, then exploded in a blue lightning storm whose bolts reached out, tore a gaping hole in the alloy wall, and sent shock waves rumbling through the ground as we dropped for cover.

"Rooslin? Copy?" I repeated. "Rooslin?"

Javelin clambered in front of me. "Sir! We're locked. We have to move!"

I swore, hustled my way to the wall, with Javelin and Fanjeaux falling in behind, particle rifles at the ready. We reached the southeast corner of the building, and I hazarded a glance around that corner. Clear.

"I wouldn't be here if you had followed orders," I told Javelin, my voice low and steely. "I'd be up at my tent, which wouldn't have been blown up. And now I can't reach the XO."

"Sir, I'd be happy to debate this after we obtain our objective."

"Oh, we'll be talking. And you won't be happy." I cleared the skin near my face so he could see my blackest look. "Let's go!"

We stole our way along the east side of the building, darting between walkways, knee walls, and low-lying shrubs until we neared another entrance where four Marines had set up a bunker using lightweight alloy blast plates to create a silvery carapace behind which they had manned their big guns. Artillery fire from one of our guns had blown apart the shield, and "smart schrap" from the shell had ignited to repeatedly poke at the Marines' combat skins like a billion tiny, sharp-edged jackhammers making one hundred thrusts per second. Their remains, covered by pale, wet viscera, lay across the shattered blast plates.

I waved Javelin ahead of me. "Good," he said. "We'll coordinate from here."

"Get the Fourteenth and the Fifteenth out of there," I said. "Get them back to their original positions."

"Sir, I say again. The Fifty-first is getting its ass kicked in there."

"Not for long. Just get your squads. Cover us when we come out."

I started for the doors, one of them hanging half off from the blast.

"Sir, you're not going in there?" Fanjeaux asked.

"Just wait for my signal."

Javelin smiled, probably glad I wanted to take off on what he deemed a suicide run. "Yes, sir."

I stepped over the dead Marines, ducked, and forced my way past the shattered door as I heard Javelin give the order over the general frequency for the Fourteenth and Fifteenth Squads to fall back and reinforce the Sixteenth outside. With the Fiftieth Platoon back in line, all I had to worry about now were the Fifty-first and Fifty-second, whose mission was to enter admin and neutralize the enemy while attempting to cause minimal damage to the structure, no small feat to be sure.

Even as I left the door and turned right, down a corridor that would take me past a long bank of offices, I heard the muffled booming of microcharges and the closer rat-a-tat of particle fire. With the light sticks mounted on the wall either shattered or flickering, I paused, brought up a thermal view in my HUV, then reached for a Ka-Bar. The sickly sweet odor of something burning made me grimace and search for its source.

Perhaps twenty bodies lay along the corridor, some Alliance Marines, others green recruits from my own company. The computer zoomed in on each of the casualties, identified the victim, then noted the loss in our central database. Familiar names flashed again and again, the computer now a beacon of death holding me in its light. Nearly every member of the Seventeenth Squad lay in the hall, incinerated by the Western Alliance's latest toy: a silent laser rifle that dismembered you with surgical precision. For nearly all of my people, this had been their first and last combat experience. As the centuries-old superstition dictated, you died either at the beginning of your service or at the very end . . .

I found my mouth opening, words coming in a gasp, "Oh my God . . ." In all the chaos, I had failed to keep close tabs on the number of troops I was losing.

Someone rounded the corner ahead. I tensed, shrinking to my knees. My HUV zoomed in, IDed the soldier as Aaron Cavalier, whose surname befit him. Though he, too, was about as green as his people, he had taken on the responsibility of commanding three squads with a chilly detachment that had infuriated me. Recently, I had become nervous when a rumor reached my desk about his using "jaca," a synthetic narcotic that hides itself from detection. I had offered him a subtle warning about "medications," and he had simply yessed me to death. Young Mr. Cavalier had no idea of what he would face, and the fact that he seemed to breeze through his life, numbed perhaps by drug use, made me believe all the more that his rude awakening would strike a much harder blow than it did to the average guardsman.

Cavalier staggered down the hall, his skin down, his particle rifle hanging limply from his side. As he drew closer, I saw a burn on the side of his head—a near miss from one of those lasers. He drew closer, tripped over a corpse that had once answered to him, then fell to his knees.

"Cavalier," I called, de-skinning so he could see me better.

"Who's that?" he asked, oblivious to my approach, though I came directly toward him.

"Lieutenant, it's me." I reached him, grabbed his wrist, helped him to his feet, dragged him toward the wall.

He furrowed his brow, spoke in a weird lilt. "Oh, yeah. The captain. The big man. Got the Racinian conditioning. Got the superhuman alien parasites in your head. Trying to save the galaxy before you become an old man, so they say. Got the big command going. Trying to stay alive so you can make sure they spell your name right in the history logs but lookin' kinda depressed and makin' me think that maybe, just maybe, who knows, maybe you want to die."

I grabbed him by the neck. "Lieutenant, where's the rest of your platoon?"

He returned a zombie's stare. I shoved him away, took off running down the corridor. "Computer? Can you locate Captain Halitov yet?"

"Negative."

It took me about five minutes to get down two levels to the offices of South Point's Honors College, where, according to my tactical computer, the rest of Cavalier's platoon had become pinned down by roughly three squads of Marines. I crouched before a pair of glass doors, chanced a quick look:

A maze of corridors and offices inside made for an urban combat environment that even the most experienced troops would dread. By the time your computer told you a Marine was hidden behind a desk, that Marine would already be dodging from cover and firing.

Tight quarters or not, I was responsible for every soldier crouching within that maze, and the fact that the Marines were tightening their perimeter, getting ready to flush them out, turned that sense of responsibility into a deafening roar to help them.

I got on Cavalier's command frequency. "Sergeant Canada? Copy?"

"Copy, sir," said the young woman whom I imagined poised behind some piece of furniture, her short, brown hair damp with sweat, her narrow green eyes pleading. "I don't know what's wrong with the LT. But he just . . . he just walked away."

"Copy, Sergeant. You got command."

"Sir?"

"In about ten seconds, you're going to be surrounded. I want you to push all three squads back, toward the main entrance, north side. Get them into the stairwell and get them out of here."

"We're falling back, sir?"

"Affirmative. Now go!"

"Aye-aye, sir!"

Even as she barked the orders to her people, particle fire from the Marines cut loose with an echoing report that would've driven any de-skinned combatant to his knees, clutching his ears.

Knife in hand, I opened the door, ran forward, reached an intersection in the corridor, glanced right, left, locked gazes with a Marine kneeling against the wall, not more than two meters away.

Even as he fired, I ran to the wall, up it, tipping sideways on my own volition and coming over him. I doubted he had ever seen a conditioned soldier because my maneuver so stunned him that he broke fire, turned, and gaped up at me as I dropped on him, driving my Ka-Bar past his combat skin and into his gut. The fact that I was able to penetrate his skin with a mere blade further surprised him, and that was probably his last thought, accompanied by a horrible sting I knew all too well.

To describe the next thirty minutes in gutwrenching detail would, some argue, be cathartic. Not for me. Suffice it to say that all but three of my people got out while I summarily and unceremoniously killed all twenty-two enemy Marines. Were it not for my combat skin, my hands, arms, chest, and legs would've been soaked in blood. How many parents, brothers, sisters, husbands, wives, and children would cry because of what I had done?

When I was finished, I hit the stairwell, taking the steps two at a time. I reached the first floor landing, seized the door, swung it toward me.

A Marine guarding that door from the other side whirled, brought his rifle to bear on me while jamming his boot into the door.

I groped for the bond, believing I could find the particles between me, the air, and the rounds soon to explode from his muzzle. I would apply force to those rounds, to that bead, bend the stream back toward him like a garden hose that would spray into his face. I had seen Major Yakata perform a similar feat, and I had employed the same technique on Gatewood-Callista. Before the Marine would realize what was happening, his own rounds would have gnawed into his combat skin, then his flesh and bone and brain.

The rounds came, all right, striking my combat skin squarely in the chest and driving back toward the opposite wall. I dodged right, reached the wall. Dodged left, hit another wall. I started for the staircase.

Then a sudden boom reverberated through the well. The Marine's skin sparked, veins of energy fingered their way across his shoulders, then the skin darkened and sloughed off. A strange look came over his face as the rifle fell from his hand, and he collapsed a second later, revealing Battalion Commander Disque, clutching a smart schrap grenade launcher, smoke rising from its muzzle.

"Captain, I want you topside. I want what's left of Zodiac Company stationed along the perimeter. Grid points should already be uploaded. We'll talk about this fuck up later."

"Yeah, Yankee Company'll mop up your mess," said Derick Kohrana, Yankee's captain and company commander. He slipped in behind Disque, clearing his skin to reveal girlish lips and a face that looked pretty, even while twisted in disgust. I barely knew Kohrana, heard he was quite a womanizer with those big eyelashes and smooth line of bullshit. I hated him. He went on: "I don't know why everybody thinks these conditioned guys are the way to go. I really don't."

"You can stow that and get your platoons in here," Disque told him. "Now!" Kohrana left, then Disque faced me, gaze still flaming. "What the fuck are you waiting for?"

"Sir!" I hustled around him, into the hall, and jogged by a long line of guardsmen from Yankee Company double-timing in the opposite direction. "Computer? Location of Captain Halitov?"

"Unknown."

"Set alert if his tac comes back on-line."

"Alert set."

I had no idea what the hell had happened to my friend, and his absence made me realize just how much I had come to depend on him, not just as a fiercely loyal XO, but as the last vestige of my old life, of my early days at the academy, of a time when both of us had been blithely unaware of what was to come. I remember the night my brother Jarrett had told me he was dropping out of the academy. He represented home to me, and his leaving meant that I would no longer be safe.

As I ran down that hall, I felt just as vulnerable as I had that night at the academy. Rooslin was gone. After Jarrett, Rooslin had been my home. Now I was the only one left.

Much to my chagrin, Yankee Company managed to neutralize the Marines inside the admin building. In fact, within six hours, our battalion, along with two others, took control of the academy grounds. Thankfully, Disque was so busy with logistical concerns that he had, thus far, not had the time to tear me a new orifice for my company's failure.

With our atmoattack jets streaking overhead in a clear display that we also controlled the skies, I sat on a collapsible chair outside my new command tent, waiting for my second lieutenants to report, waiting for my computer to tell me something, anything, about Halitov.

Javelin came loping over, stood at attention. "Sir, reporting for debriefing, sir!"

"At ease. Get two more chairs out of the tent. Bring them out here."

Not thrilled by the errand boy task, Javelin groaned, "Aye-aye, sir."

He disappeared into the dusty brown hemisphere that blended into the landscape. Second Lieutenants Aaron Cavalier and Grace Thomason arrived, Cavalier still appearing only half-present, Thomason brooding over something that seemed to turn her dark skin even darker. Her nostrils flared as she met my gaze, snapped off a salute, gave the standard acknowledgment, then turned her big brown eyes away.

Javelin returned with the chairs, and I gestured that the three take seats. Javelin and Thomason were clearly bewildered by my informality, which was, of course, lost on Cavalier.

"So we fucked up today," I began.

"And you want to sit around and chat about it, sir?" asked Javelin.

"As a matter of fact I do."

Javelin nodded, decided to press another button: "Sir, have they located Captain Halitov's body yet?"

"Captain Halitov is still MIA. Presumed alive."

"That the official word?"

"That's *my* word."

"Sir, permission to speak off the record, sir?" asked Thomason.

"Go ahead."

"Halitov's probably dead. I lost nearly half my platoon. Cavalier lost even more. And for what, sir?"

"Not glory," said Javelin as he widened his gaze on me. " 'Cause like you said, we fucked up. Sir."

"I got drafted into this, made an officer just 'cause I

got a college degree," Thomason said. "You know, at first, I really thought we were doing something noble. Fighting for what you said—a just and lasting peace. The alliances have been exploiting the colonies for far too long. But sir, Scott . . . it's all bullshit, man. It's just about money. And land. Our side is as corrupt as theirs, but at least they're going to win. They have more resources, more personnel. Period. I watched so many of my people die today, and I'm just . . . I don't know if I can do this. It's more than just morally and ethically wrong. It's suicide."

There I sat, looking at them, my command staff: a pain in my ass know-it-all, an unconfirmed junkie, and a conscientious objector. For a second, I wished I were back on Gatewood-Callista, in charge of my platoon. I actually wished that Sergeant Mai Lan, mutinous bitch though she had been, was working with me. She hated my guts and thought I was wrong about everything, but she had been far more capable than any of these people. Javelin was a noncommissioned officer who had cashed in on the war's demand for personnel by lobbying hard for his commission. Cavalier, like Thomason, came from the farms of Tau Ceti XI, where he had earned his degree in agriculture, then had received the word: you're drafted. Dodging the draft was punishable by a long prison sentence, even death in extreme cases. I should have sympathized more with those two, but they weren't like me, soldiers who wanted to find out what duty, honor, and courage really mean. Thomason had once told me that she was not supposed to be shouting at troops. She was supposed to be teaching high school science to a class of bright-eyed young colos. Cavalier just wanted to be out in the fields, with his crops, figuring out new ways to yield even more food. Perhaps the violence of war, standing in such sharp relief to a field of corn nodding in the breeze, had driven Cavalier to find an escape through hallucinogens. I vowed that before we left Exeter, he would come clean with me, or I would do everything in my power to get him discharged. I had already debriefed him privately, had stripped away his command and given it to his platoon sergeant, but that hadn't seemed to faze him.

"Sir, did you hear what I said?" Thomason asked.

"Yeah. And sorry, Lieutenant, but I'm not in the mood to change your mind."

That hoisted her brows.

"You three think Halitov and I don't have enough experience for this command. Yeah, maybe you heard about what we pulled on Gatewood-Callista, how many Marines we took out, but I know you still don't think we're capable. Truth is, none of us is ready for this. And I'm not sure there's any amount of training that can prepare you for what we've seen. But here we are, in the shit. And we will make the best of it because I'm in command. No other reason. We won't decide on our own who needs help and who doesn't. We won't reinterpret orders to suit ourselves. We won't suddenly decide in the middle of combat that our political biases and agenda have changed and that maybe it's not right to kill these people anymore. Finally, we won't numb ourselves to the world. We're going to keep our minds clear and do our jobs. You fucked up inside because you didn't trust in me. I'm making the decisions. I'm not going to hesitate. I'm not going to steer you wrong. And if I ever do, I'm going to pay for it with my life. You can count on that. Now that's the end of my little heart-to-heart. Comments?"

Cavalier's chin slowly lifted. "When are we gonna eat?"

I was about to lean over, grab him by the ear, and shake him until all that garbage in his head oozed out and allowed him to return to us, but Lieutenant Colonel Disque came marching up the hill, toward our powwow.

Javelin glanced at the lieutenant colonel. "Shit. Are we dismissed, sir?"

"Dismissed."

"Captain St. Andrew," Disque called, singing my name in a tune that might as well be my funeral hymn. "Finished debriefing your three losers?"

I rose, snapped to, and issued my salute, as my people practically ran off. "Sir, my platoon leaders have been debriefed, sir."

"At ease, Captain," he said, then dropped heavily into one of the chairs Javelin had failed to pack away. "You know on my way up here, I passed this long line of glad bags, and I have to tell you, most of the bodies stuffed in them were from your company. You dropped in here with a hundred and sixty-two. What do you got left, son?"

I sat, cleared my throat. "Sir, roll stands tall at eighty-nine, sir."

"Stands tall? Are you kidding me? They condition a fuckin' gennyboy, somehow he gets ahold of a company, loses his XO, loses nearly half his people. Jesus Christ!"

My brother's words haunted me once more: *You'll*

always be a gennyboy first, an officer second. The only way you'll get respect is by earning it through what you do— and even then they'll talk behind your back. I'm telling you this because you're my brother. You have to hear it.

Every muscle in my body tightened, and I imagined myself throttling the lieutenant colonel right there. He had called me gennyboy, and I could report him for that. But he knew I wouldn't start that fire between us.

"Sir, I have a morale problem, and I am—"

"Of course you got a morale problem. We all got one. These kids have been ripped away from their homes. We've shoved weapons into their hands and told them to fight. But you got it even worse because they don't relate to you."

"Because I'm a gennyboy."

"Being a mining kid is one thing, but between the epi and the conditioning, you're not quite human to them. What're you going to do about that?"

"Sir, I don't know, sir."

Disque leaned back in his chair, cradled his head in his hands. "Well, you better think about it. And let me tell you something: you can't run around playing fuckin' Superman every time your company screws up. You have to teach them right, stand back, and let them do their jobs. What you did, going in there, taking out all those troops . . . yeah, you got your people out, but you didn't learn a goddamned thing about being a commander. You cheated your way out of the situation."

"But sir—"

"You hate me, but I'm willing to bet that I'm one of the only guys you're going to meet who actually gives a crap about your character as an officer. You got it hard, St. Andrew. No doubt about it. Brother killed. Birthmark on your face. Getting a little gray there in the temples because of your fucked-up conditioning . . . I don't envy you. Not at all. I do, however, envy the fact that you got a friend in a high place. I just received a communiqué from the office of Mary Brooks. We're setting up a Hunter-Killer Platoon, sending them into the Minsalo Caves to weed out any Alliance presence still there. They want you to lead it. Maybe you've been in those caves before, but I still don't think you're ready."

"Sir, I am ready."

"You calling me a liar?"

"Sir, no, sir. Just offering a different opinion, sir."

"We'll see." He stood, accidentally knocked over his chair, then picked it up. "Fuckin' military issue."

I stood, found it hard to meet his scrutinizing gaze. "Sir, would you like me to put together a command team?"

"You know, if I had any say in this, you wouldn't be going."

"I understand, sir."

"I'll put together your team, throw in your three platoon commanders, whom I know you get along with so well. And I'll make Kohrana your XO. He'll keep you honest."

My shoulders slumped a little. "Yes, sir."

"One more thing. Off the record. What do you think happened to Halitov? He's MIA, but . . . think he went AWOL?"

"Sir, no, sir."

"Every corpse but his has been accounted for. Air search has nothing. What do you think?"

"Sir, Captain Halitov would not go AWOL."

He studied me. "Then he'd best be dead, because no one deserts on my watch. No one."

3 ❯ **Disque had been** trying to teach me something in that meeting, but I hadn't been listening. I would earn the respect of my people if I listened
to them carefully, then allowed them to find creative
solutions to problems. I needed to let them do their
jobs and not rush in to save the day. I had failed because I had wanted too badly to win. And I still didn't
know how to accept and learn from my failures. I kept
wanting to win because, well, that was easy . . .

The strange disappearance of Captain Rooslin Halitov became a popular topic of conversation, second
only to war news tawted in from Kennedy-Centauri.
While the remainder of my company rotated on
watch duty but otherwise enjoyed some much
needed R&R, I lay on a thin gelrack in my command
tent, listening to the familiar *ta-ta-ta* of the insects we
had nicknamed "triplets" when I had been a South
Point cadet. In the distance, an occasional round of
particle fire echoed off the mesas. That would be
troops warding off the *shraxi*, those toothy nocturnal
carnivores that emerged from their burrows and trav-
eled in threes. Though less than a meter tall when
standing on their hind legs, *shraxi* could take down a
man in just a few moments. They were nasty crea-
tures, but I didn't mind them as much as I could have.
Their presence, the cool, dry air, and the music of the
triplets swept me away from all the stress. I needed to

relax. In just a few hours I'd be traveling via Armored Troop Carrier out to the caves. I imagined I was just a first year again, having only to worry about my studies and physical training.

My tac beeped. I swore, sat up, activated my HUV, and took the incoming call, which originated from the SSGC *Auspex*, in orbit with six other troop transports as well as nine capital ships and their support vessels. It was odd that the caller was not identified, but when I saw who it was shimmering ghostlike in the display, I knew why.

"Hello, again," said Captain Kristi Breckinridge, wearing her unflappable game face. "I understand you're heading out to the Minsalo Caves in the morning."

"That's classified."

"I have a message for you from Colonel Beauregard. He asks that you do everything possible to find his son."

I wondered what was really going on with the brass: I already felt like a pawn, and Beauregard's message only confirmed that. "Disque told me he got orders from Ms. Brooks. Is that true? Did the colonel twist some arms to get me in there?"

"I can't say. And you do, of course, have another mission to accomplish. I understand X-Ray Company's going out there to secure the conditioning facility."

"That's correct."

"You know they're wasting their time, right? The alliances never got the facility back on-line. According to our intel, that quake caused irreparable damage."

"If that's true, then you and the rest of the Wardens

just sat around watching the Seventeen waste resources."

"If I'm the colonel, wasting the Seventeen's resources
is not a huge sacrifice—if I can retrieve my son."

"Does he know how many people died here? And
for what? It's not like there's anything of real value,
now that you're saying the conditioning facility can't
be repaired."

"What about the caves themselves?"

"What about them?"

"If the colonel's son is there, and Dina is with
him . . . I mean, if she's alive . . ."

"You don't believe those caves can bring people
back from the dead, do you?"

"You told me you'd been healed by them yourself."

"Healed, yeah. Resurrected? No."

"Well, I hope you find out in the morning. Last
thing: the colonel will honor your request to have
Halitov reconditioned, with the understanding that
once he is, he becomes a Colonial Warden."

"Oh, he understands how blackmail works. He understands it as clearly as you do."

She rolled her eyes. "I'm offering both of you *life*.
Have you checked the news lately? All of the original
Sol colonies have fallen. Forget Mars. Forget all of Sol.
The alliances are beginning a major push outward.
They're going to leapfrog from system to system, se-
curing each as they go along. Rumor has it they're
getting ready to stage a major offensive at Kennedy-
Centauri. The colonial capital will fall if the Wardens
don't intervene. Like it or not, that is the way it is."

"Are we done?"

"Not yet. Why are you lying to me about Halitov?"

"Lying?"

"You think I don't have access? He's listed MIA."

"I never said he wasn't."

"Scott, as much as you don't like me, I'm here to help you. I'm a resource. We have several people down there who are looking for him right now."

My tone softened a little. "Really?"

"Alive or dead, we'll find him."

"Thank you."

"Sounds like you still don't trust me."

"Say hi to your brother for me." I cut the link, imagining the fire in her eyes. Then I sat there, thinking about my friend. *Rooslin, what happened to you?*

"Sir?" cried Platoon Sergeant Canada from just outside my tent. "Sorry to disturb you, sir. But we got a problem!"

I came out of the tent, saw her standing there, face illumined by the light stick in her fist. "What is it, Sergeant?"

"It's Lieutenant Cavalier, sir." She turned, pointed outward. "There."

Out in the distance, atop one of the smaller cliffs within Virginis Canyon, stood Second Lieutenant Cavalier. I immediately skinned up, zoomed in on him for a better look. He was naked, arms outstretched against the great silhouettes of rock and the dusty curtain of stars. His head lolled back, his eyes closed, and his mouth fell open, as though in ecstasy. He stood mere inches from the sheer drop-off, the canyon floor a dizzying three hundred meters below. I de-skinned. "Airjeep! Now!"

"They're on patrol. It's going to take a few minutes, sir."

"How the hell did he get up there?" I said, breaking into a jog toward the canyon.

"I don't know. Maybe he bribed an MP to drop him off."

Privates from Yankee Company positioned along the barracks' perimeter began fanning out from their posts, drawing closer to the cliff for a better look.

As I neared the canyon, I still couldn't believe that one of my officers stood atop a wall of mottled strata that we cadets had called Whore Face, because of her good hand- and footholds. It appeared one of my officers was going to commit suicide on my old training ground.

"How long on that airjeep, Sergeant?" I hollered.

"Couple minutes."

We reached the canyon floor directly below Cavalier, and I had to skin up to see his face. "Cavalier!" His name echoed off into the night. He didn't react.

I swept my gaze down, across the rock, all the way to the floor. Three hundred meters. If the quantum bond remained true, I could scale that in a few heartbeats, make it up top, maybe talk him down. But if the bond failed, even my skin wouldn't save me. I'd rebound until most of my bones were broken. Was his life worth the risk?

Trembling with indecision, I stared once more at him, actually smiled as I thought, *It's just a dream. After that call from Breckinridge, I fell back asleep, and this is just a dream. I don't have to feel guilty about not trying to save this guy . . .*

"I think he's going to jump, sir," said Canada, as

Cavalier wormed a little closer to the edge, dirt dropping off from his toes, now hanging in the air.

"Jesus God, what do we got now?" boomed Disque as he marched up beside me. My bad luck placed the lieutenant-colonel's command tent only a hundred meters away.

"I think he's hallucinating, sir," Canada said.

"Oh, really? Thought he was just taking the family jewels for a walk," Disque retorted, then he skinned up, set the volume on his voice way up to mimic an old-fashioned bullhorn. "Lieutenant, what in God's name are you doing on my cliff?"

It was all I could do to remain there and listen to Lieutenant-colonel Jesus work his "subtle persuasion" on Cavalier.

"Son, I asked you a question," Disque shouted, now even more incensed.

Without another thought, I just did it, ran like I was on fire, found the bond, exploited the hell out of it, and began sprinting up the canyon wall as though it were the floor.

"Holy shit," Disque cried. I wanted to believe he'd seen other conditioned officers in action, but a feat of this magnitude had probably never reached his eyes.

All right, so I did trip over a few pitons jutting from the rock. Those little metal spikes had been left over from all our training exercises, but they didn't stop me from reaching the top and rounding the corner about four meters away from Cavalier, who still hadn't opened his eyes.

Tentatively, I stepped toward him. "Aaron. Hey, man. I'm right over here."

"You think I want to die?" he asked, then began

chuckling to himself. "That why you think I'm up here?"

"One of my officers strips naked, stands at the edge of a cliff, and I'm thinking he wants to jump. Call me crazy."

"St. Andrew, get that idiot away from the edge right now!" ordered Disque.

"Sir, yes, sir!" I boomed halfheartedly.

"I love it," said Cavalier. "All this attention, me right here on the edge, surrounded by nature. I love it. This place, this moon, Exeter . . . it's alive. It knows I'm here. It's aware of me. And I *mean* something to it, just like right now, I mean something to all of you. My life matters."

Blinding lights wiped past me, shone in my eyes a second as an airjeep rose from the canyon, hovered a few meters away from us. An MP rose from the passenger's seat, aimed a CZX Forty antigrav rifle at Cavalier. "Lieutenant, stand down!"

"Hey, I got this," I shouted to the MP.

"It's a security problem now, Captain," barked the MP.

"Aaron, they're going to hit you with the CZX to make sure you don't jump. You know what that's going to feel like. Just move back from the edge."

"No, I'm going to stay here, and I'm going to be important, and my life's going to really matter, and people are going to remember me. That's what I'm going to do. That's what's going to happen."

A quick hiss, and the MP fired—but the weapon's beam did not lock on to and encase Cavalier in its energy. The MP had misadjusted the power setting, and the beam blasted Cavalier over the edge.

I gasped, slid out toward the drop-off, saw him dropping away, heard his cry . . .

And one, two, three, I leapt over the side, after him.

In those days, I considered myself pretty damned foolish because only a fool would throw himself off a cliff knowing that the bond, his only safety net was, at best, unreliable.

Then again, that wasn't the first time I had literally jumped off a cliff. Before I was conditioned, I had fallen from that very wall and been saved by Sergeant Pope. Clearly, the universe was toying with me, amusing itself through my angst and its repetition of time and place.

About halfway down, I knew I'd be all right. The bond surged within me. But about halfway down, I also realized that I would not reach Cavalier in time, and no one below had a CZX to save him. He hit the ground, back first, and his entire body snapped like a twig and went limp. I hit the deck, bent my knees, and my skin tapered off as I willed myself away from the bond.

A handful of grunts gaped at me, finding more interest in my jump than in Cavalier's death. I rushed to my lieutenant, checked his neck for a carotid pulse. No pulse. No chance.

"All right, everyone, back to your posts," ordered Disque. "Louis, get a detail in here to"—he made a face at Cavalier's broken body—"take care of this."

Louis, a sergeant from Yankee Company, saluted and activated his tac.

Disque came over, and, surprisingly, put a hand on my shoulder. "Son," he began quietly, almost sympathetically, "your people . . . they're dropping like flies."

"Bad joke, sir," I said, my gaze not straying from Cavalier.

"Yeah," Disque said. "Bad joke."

At 0600 local time, X-Ray, Yankee, and Zodiac Companies piled into admin's war-torn primary assembly hall for a nondenominational memorial service in honor of our fallen comrades. The regimental commander, Vivian Hurly, read a little speech from the screen of a palm-sized tablet, while we stood in formation. I noted that we had heard the quote-laden speech at least twice before. There was nothing personal, nothing uniquely passionate about words she would continue to recycle. Disque, of course, also went through the motions, though he did shock some of us and his superiors, when, at the close of his brief remarks, he said, "A lot of people died here—but we still kicked fuckin' ass. Remember that!"

Those not shocked included the back row of grunts, most from Yankee Company, who cheered and repeated his message at the tops of their lungs until squad corporals evil-eyed them into silence.

After the service, we ate, though I couldn't stomach much more than a piece of toast and some lukewarm coffee. I met up with Canada, who now officially assumed Cavalier's spot, and we headed out to the airfield. Javelin and Thomason had already gone off to fetch our gear from the supply sergeant.

We took a path overlooking the academy grounds from about a hundred meters up. I had taken the route many times during my cadet days. Thin columns of smoke still rose from the barracks where X-Ray Company had taken on Marines dug in between the buildings. Still more smoke rose from the library and classroom buildings, both of which had sustained major damage from artillery fire. The longer I looked out at the academy, the more depressed I felt. The training ground of my cadet days— a place where we had all been wonderfully naive and untouched by war—was vanishing before my eyes.

"Sir, I, uh, I wanted to, now that we have a moment, I wanted to talk you about . . ." Canada sighed against her stammering.

"What is it, Sergeant?"

"So I'm officially in charge of the Fifty-first now."

"I'll have your star in hand right after this Op."

"So I really get the star, all ten points, just like that?"

"Are you kidding me? Yesterday, I was a cadet. After this place got invaded, and we made it out, they gave me my commission, a platoon, and sent me home to Gatewood-Callista. My first platoon mutinied on me. So they made me a captain and gave me Zodiac Company." I grinned over the irony. "I love the Seventeen."

"Sir, I'm not ready."

"You think I was? You think I am? They can dump all the information they want into your brain, but data can never replace real experience happening in real time. The tech guys will argue with me there, tell me that data contains experiences, memories that will seem as real as any others. But there's always a little voice in my head that tells me you never did this, you never learned that. It's just the cerebro. They can't erase your doubt without erasing you."

"Which is why I'm not ready."

"Which is the reason why you're perfect for the job.

You're a clean slate, ready to be molded into a powerful and decisive officer based on very real combat experiences. You'll be okay."

"Thanks for the vote of confidence, but I know you're desperate for personnel."

"We're all desperate, and the shortage will get worse if we don't have good leaders."

"You think I'll be a good leader?"

"You're from Aire-Wu."

"What's that supposed to mean?"

"The narrative in your folder says that four generations of your family have worked in the timber industry there. Butanee was it?"

"Yeah, but lumberjacks don't make for good leaders. Trust me. We're all bush people, like to be alone, and we do not want anyone micromanaging us."

"I grew up in a mine. We traded in ore. Miners and lumberjacks are cut from the same cloth. And you'd be surprised how well we adapt to leading and being led."

"I would be. Because right now I feel pretty lost. I mean, everyone knows Cavalier was taking something. How am I supposed to get my people past that? What if Cavalier wasn't the only junkie? What then?"

"You'll deal with it. We both will."

"How can you be so confident?"

"Because this is my company. And no one, I mean no one, is going to let me down. If it makes you feel better, just keep telling yourself you *are* ready. It's a pretty good lie. It works for me. Most of the time."

"Aye-aye, sir."

"And Canada? One last bit of advice. I'm sharing all my fears and doubts with you, and to be honest, that's not the way to play it with your people. If they see you're afraid, if they see you're indecisive, they will not follow. Everybody hates Disque. But most of us would follow him to our deaths. I'm not saying you have to be a prick. Just calm. Always assessing the situation and reacting like that." I snapped my fingers. She nodded.

We walked a few more moments in silence, me thinking about the fact that she came from Aire-Wu and remembering that the second conditioning facility was supposedly there. Eventually I asked, "Sergeant, in all the time you were home before you got drafted, and believe me, I know Aire-Wu's a big planet, but just out of curiosity, did you ever see any military presence there that seemed, I don't know, unusual?"

I paused to read her expression, and, strangely enough, she looked a little nervous. "What do you mean? The Seventeen's always had a base in Butanee."

"Never mind. Forget it."

"Wait. So everybody thinks the Racinians terraformed my world, and there are always research projects going on to learn the truth. We even had guys digging in the middle of one of our tree farms, not too far from a few of the mills. I remember those lab coat guys were escorted by military people. Is that what you're talking about?"

"Maybe. Did they ever find anything?"

"I don't know. If they did, they never told us about it. They paid my dad a lot for the okay to dig, though. Stayed there a few months, filled in the holes, and pulled out. Why do you ask?"

"Just following up on something. Thanks."

"And thank you, sir. I mean for the advice."

"Anytime."

"Oh, I almost forgot to ask. Any word about the XO?"

I shook my head.

"It's like someone just plucked him off the battle-field."

My voice grew thin. "Yeah, it is."

We neared the tarmac, and abruptly the solitude of the path and stillness of the morning yielded sharply to the whine of warming turbines, the faint howl of the wind sweeping down from the mesas, and the hollering of squad corporals. About fifty yards ahead, Javelin, Thomason, and Kohrana loaded backpacks into the cargo hold of a G21 Endosector Armored Troop Carrier, one of two quad-winged birds of prey that would carry our three squads to the caves. Since it was a special operation, officers were supposed to pitch in as much as the grunts, and I was glad to see my command team pulling their weight. I had fig-ured that Javelin and Kohrana would dole out the grunt work to, well, the grunts. Still, they had not taken the entire burden of loading upon themselves. A half dozen privates stocked the other ATC while the rest shifted in single file into the hold.

"Captain," Kohrana said, looking up from an un-derwing cargo bay and backhanding sweat from his brow. "Thanks for dropping by."

"Is our gear stowed, XO?" I asked, all business and denying him a reaction to his remark.

"Yes, sir. The gear is stowed. Almost finished boarding."

"Very well. Alert the pilots. Dust off at their discre-tion."

Canada and I left him and headed up the gangway, into the hold. I took a jumpseat between her and Javelin. Opposite us sat privates zippered into black combat utilities that hardened the appearance of even the prettiest young women. A shudder broke through me as, for a moment, I spotted a grunt who looked a little like Dina. I closed my eyes.

"Sir, all present and accounted for," said Kohrana. I jolted as he took a seat opposite me and lowered the big safety bars over his shoulders. He clipped the stock of his QQ90 particle rifle into the deck mount between his legs. "Dust off in thirty seconds," he reported.

The turbines cycled up, and all that raw power rumbled through the hold for a full half minute until we rose in a vertical takeoff. I switched on my tac and let Disque know that we were en route and would issue status reports as necessary. He gave me the unwelcome news that several Western Alliance capital ships had just tawted into orbit and were squaring off with our fleet. His advice was as crude as it was curt: "Haul major fucking ass. Read me, Captain?"

"Loud and clear, sir!"

The first Racinian ruins on Exeter had been discovered inside the Minsalo Caves, and I knew more about them than most of my colleagues. My dad was a geologist, and maybe it was in my genes, but most of my life I've had a special interest in rock formations, sedimentary layers, and, well, dirt. Not the most interesting stuff, but I like the idea that rocks are like history books, though their stories rarely lie and are not influenced by personal agendas. There may not be any more pure form of history.

The caves' colossal entrance hung on a cliff wall nearly six hundred meters above Virginis Canyon's dry riverbed. The first time I had come to the place, we had been forced to rappel down the cliff, then pendulum ourselves inside the cave. Our entry via the ATCs would be far less dangerous and dramatic. I watched from a small window as the first ship hovered near that great open mouth of stone, turned tail, and backed up toward the cave. The gangway came down, and even as it made contact with the cave floor, my guardsmen flooded out, their skins set to a fluctuating camouflage of red, brown, and alabaster-white that mirrored the colors of the cave walls. I skinned up myself, called on my HUV, and watched a digitized image of them dispersing.

"Captain, First and Second Squads are in," reported Squad Sergeant Hurley, one of Kohrana's people from Yankee Company.

"Copy that, Sergeant. Establish your perimeter points down to the Great Hall. Copy?"

"Copy, sir."

"You meet any resistance, you take them out."

"Yes, sir."

"So, Captain, rumor has it you've been here before," said Kohrana, as the ATC banked hard, then began lining up its tail with the entrance.

"That's no rumor. And here's a tip: most of this place isn't on the map. Somebody gets lost, all that rock could interfere with GPS signals and transponders. So let's keep everyone buddied up and tight."

"Does it ever bother you?" he asked suddenly, fingering his own cheek and staring at the birthmark on mine. "I mean, does it itch or anything?"

Before I could answer, the hold's gangway began yawning open, and our safety bars automatically whined up and away.

"All right," cried Mazamo, a stocky blond woman and Third Squad's sergeant. "Ready on the line. By the numbers. Just like the drill."

The troops formed a neat line, with the first poised at the red mark near the gangway's edge.

At that moment, I couldn't help but launch into one of Sergeant Pope's old morale boosters. "Squad, are you ready?"

"Yes, sir!" they boomed.

"Very well. Go! Go! Go!"

One after another they jogged down the ramp, leapt onto the cave's dusty stone floor, and fanned out. I unclipped my own particle rifle from the floor and fell in behind Javelin, Thomason, Canada, and Kohrana.

We were in the cave no more than a few seconds when the echo of particle fire sounded ahead, from where the entrance funneled down into a narrow gallery. I darted to a wall, hunkered down, and read the screens in my HUV. "Hurley? Report?"

"Snipers. Hit-and-run. Think we wounded one of them, but we got one dead, two wounded ourselves."

"Get them up here." I looked to Kohrana. "Medevac."

He nodded and made the call while I studied a 3-D map of the entrance. As expected, those Alliance snipers were jamming my HUV and effectively con-

cealing themselves from detection. The fact they had
detected us meant that they had either made visual
contact, or someone had given them our encryption
codes so they could detect our communications or tac
signals. Whatever the case, we had lost the element of
surprise, and they might even be tracking us.

"Medevac's en route, but are you sure you don't
want to leave them?" asked Kohrana. "Let the magic
caves do their work?"

I matched his cynical grin with one of my own.
"No."

"Got another question. If the caves heal people,
then every time we shoot the enemy, he lies down
and gets healed. Then he's ready for more. So we
can't kill him."

"And maybe he can't kill us."

"This is nuts."

I chuckled under my breath. "Now you're making
sense."

"What if we dismember them? You think the caves
can put bodies back together?"

"Forget that. Let's establish where we are: they're
expecting us and regrouping, trying to reinforce their
positions, which is why we're going in now, full
force."

"You're insane. We'll draw too much fire."

"Hey, man. When they're shooting at you, they're
telling you where they are."

"Screw that. We have to—"

"First, Second, Third Squads?" I called, getting
quickly to my feet. "Hard and fast. Flush them out.
Let's go!" I took off toward the gallery, leaving a
stunned Kohrana in my wake.

"You can't do this," he cried.

"I know," I called back. "I'm insane. Follow me!"
Though I never glanced back, I suspected the color
had faded from his cheeks.

4

I raced by one of the markers left several decades prior by a speleological team. The little hemisphere had been flashing all that time, marking the path. The tunnel grew more narrow, a lot more damp, then, as I remembered, it sloped down in a thirty-five-degree grade, with the ceiling just a meter above my head. More gunfire punctuated the whistling wind and quickened my pace.

"Captain?" gasped Kohrana, trying to keep up with me. "You're taking us right into those snipers!"

"Like you said, they'll all just get shot and healed. Either way, we got no time for cat and mouse. There's an Alliance fleet in orbit. We have to flush out these Marines and get the hell out of here." There was another thing I wanted to do, but he didn't need to know about that.

"If the Alliance is going to win back this moon, then who cares if we do this?" asked Thomason, who had obviously been monitoring my command channel. "We've already lost."

"We don't know what's going to happen up there, so we do our jobs. And we do them quickly. Canada, you copy?"

"Yes, sir! Just hitting the Great Hall now. Jesus, this place is big. Lots of stalagmites for them to set up sniper nests."

"Move in, three by three. Close proximity. Tight to

the wall. Listen to Hurley. He knows what he's doing. And set your particle range for two meters, nearly point-blank. You're going to have ricocheting like you wouldn't believe if you open up."

"Copy that, sir. Seen some already. Moving out."

"Javelin? You with me?" I called, waited, was about to call again when:

"I'm here, Captain. There's another tunnel about ten meters ahead, right near the entrance to the hall. Heads off to the right. Can't bring it up on the map, but I want to take Second Squad in there."

"Do it."

"Sir, are you sure, sir?"

"What do you mean, Lieutenant?"

"I mean, sir, this is my idea. You're going along?"

I regret what I said next. It was unprofessional, but it just came out. "Javelin, *do not* fuck with me. Get in there and kill anything that moves. Copy?"

"Uh, copy, sir."

Kohrana cleared the skin near his face to reveal his frown. "You okay?"

"Yeah, I'm okay. You people piss me off, you know that? Just hold your position."

And the fool in me took over once more. I brought my rifle to bear, scaled the wall, then, hanging inverted from the ceiling but feeling not a single graviton's pull, I bolted off for the Great Hall, negotiating around stalactites, which, from my point of view, rose from the floor.

I sprinted into the vast chamber of the Great Hall, glanced down at First Squad as they spread out, dashing from stalagmite to stalagmite, working themselves deeper into the gloomy orifice.

Then, gunfire erupted from at least a dozen points
ahead. My tactical computer immediately traced the
beads and singled out fourteen Western Alliance
Marines who had taken up positions at the far end of
the hall.

Three of Hurley's people took left flank, and another three took right. Good plan. They'd drive those
snipers away from the main exit and toward a far corner. I opted to take out the four Marines in the middle, and I'd do that quietly, before they knew what
had hit them.

The first Marine who had been firing then ducking
back behind a narrow stalagmite glanced up at the
rush of wind behind him. Exploiting the bond to penetrate his combat skin, I drove the butt of my rifle into
his face as I dropped on him. We collapsed and still
disoriented but gripping his weapon, he rolled away.

But I had already abandoned my weapon and had
the blade of my Ka-Bar sticking from the bottom of
my fist. He got a nanosecond look at me before I
punched the blade into his heart, withdrew it, and,
panting, snatched up my gun and dodged to a glossy
stalagmite a few meters to my right.

Listening only to the sound of my breathing and
trying to ignore the voice in my head that whispered,
"Murderer . . . murderer . . ." I reached the stalagmite, paused, then spotted movement just ahead,
near the next pillar of stone.

"Sir! We're taking heavy fire in here," cried Javelin
over the channel. "Request permission to A-3 them,
copy?"

"Negative." Javelin wanted to use acipalm-three
grenades, which would spread their incendiary black

goo all over the cave after exploding, killing the Marines in there by working at the subatomic level to rob the gluons from their bodies. Problem was, that same theft would also destroy a portion of the cave. Our orders dictated that we preserve as much of the rock formations and alien ruins as possible.

"Sir, I've already lost three people!" Javelin argued.

"Then fall back!"

Silence. Then, finally, "Aye-aye, sir! Wait a minute . . ."

"What is it, Javelin?"

"Sir? They've ceased fire. *They're* falling back."

"Pursue!"

"Aye-aye, sir!"

I took off running for that next pillar, got there, found nothing. "Canada?"

"Copy, sir. Got seven Marine casualties so far. Rest here are falling back."

"Very well. Let's go get them."

The next tunnel, a ragged triangle just two meters wide near the base and about three meters high, led to an abandoned Racinian hangar, a vast, empty chamber with stone walls blending seamlessly into polished metal. I met up with Kohrana near the tunnel's entrance, and he hesitated before going inside.

"Something you want to say, Captain?" I asked.

His eyes grew narrower, more menacing. "No." He hustled by and jogged off into the gloom.

We crossed the hangar without incident, reached the conduit of stone on the other side, then ducked down and shifted at double time inside. All three of our squads lay ahead, and reports from Javelin, Canada, and Thomason came in, along with further observations from the squad sergeants. After about ten minutes of hunchbacked travel, we reached a familiar cavity about five hundred meters across and ringed by a natural catwalk. The moment I caught sight of the place, I remembered the woman we had chased there, back when I had been a cadet:

Her eyes widened, the irises a weird, deep shade of red, her head haloed by that mop of coarse white hair. She shifted her gaze a little, inspected us, then spoke in a rapid fire that we could barely follow. "Toroidal Curvature of the containment field allows the formation of the mediators and the establishment of a stable family of Primal Space Time Matter particles. The main TAWT drive computers, networked in a Quantum Communication Array allow the so-called faster-than-light computations to be made, which in turn collapse the wave function of any and all present conditions. As the ship's computer observes the conditions, it in effect can answer questions before they are posed."

Jarrett frowned at me.

"Why is she reciting a page from colonial history?" asked Dina.

"And why is she wearing our utilities?" Clarion added. "Unless—"

"You're not them?" the woman cried, then grabbed Jarrett's wrist with a bony hand. "You haven't come to take me back?"

Jarrett tugged himself free. "Take you back where?"

"Better yet, who're you talking about?" I asked.

"Twenty-two-sixty-six. Mining of bauxite begins on fifth planet in Ross Two-forty-eight solar system," the woman replied, her ruby eyes going vacant. "Inte-Micro Corporation CEO Tamer Yatanaya names planet Allah-Trope and declares it retreat for Muslims persecuted by

Eastern Alliance powers. Allah-Trope becomes first off-world colony with predominately one religion. By year's end, floating research operations are dropped onto planet Epsilon Eri Three—a world entirely covered by warm oceans whose salt content is only slightly higher than Terra's. Thousands of new microorganisms discovered. Aquacultural experiments yield new food sources for a human population that now numbers twenty billion, with six billion living in Sol system colonies and nearly five billion in extrasolar settlements."

"What's the matter with you?" Jarrett asked.

"I . . . it won't . . . I can't . . ."

"Are you a cadet?" Clarion demanded.

Dina crouched down and took the woman's hand in her own. "Are you a third year? A fourth year?"

The woman's eyes glossed with tears, and as she tried to answer, Jarrett checked her pockets for anything that might reveal her identity.

Now, as I stood on the catwalk, it was clear to me that that old lady was my destiny—unless I handed myself over to Breckinridge and allowed her and the Wardens to recondition me.

"What is that down there?" asked Kohrana, staring into the vast pit before us. "I'm scanning it, and I get nothing."

With my tactical computer feeding me infrared images in my HUV, I studied the curving metallic surface, which, the first time I had seen it, reminded me of a missile's nose cone. "I don't know."

"Want to send a rappelling team in there?"

I studied the pit, and in my mind's eye I saw that old woman leap into it. I repressed a shudder. "No. We keep moving."

We forged on for another fifty or so minutes, through more modest-sized tunnels connected by more caverns of flow- and dripstone. Kohrana took lead, sweeping his rifle across the path and hugging the shadows near the wall. Feeling yet another rush of déjà vu, I tried to forget about my first journey into the caves and just listened to the skipchatter on the squad channels:

"J.T. switch to tac five, copy?"

"Going to five."

"Anything on thermal, Canada?"

"We're cold so far, copy?"

"Copy. Lowe and Rammel, you're getting too loose. Tighten those lines."

"Aye-aye, sir."

A rock dropped just behind me. Nothing large, just a stone the size of a baseball. I whirled and studied the cavern, with its dozens of dark hiding places reaching beyond my night-vision's scope. Nothing. I probed once more, looked back, saw Kohrana now some ten meters ahead and shifting left, toward a large seam in the rock wall leading to the next tunnel. I threw a final look back at the cavern, glanced up to the stalactites, which seemed to close in on me for a moment.

And that's when a cold, wet hand penetrated my skin and wrapped around my mouth, even as an arm slipped around my chest. I was dragged back, toward the cavern wall. With both hands locked on my attacker's wrist, I struggled to pry free. I could feel the bond, but I still couldn't budge the hand. That could only mean my assailant was conditioned.

"Shhh. It's me."

Suddenly, the hand slipped away, and I found myself standing in a tunnel just a meter wide. I spun, saw who had grabbed me, and the words just slipped out: "What the fuck?"

Rooslin Halitov stood there, his utilities ruffled and dripping wet, as though he'd been swimming in them. He cocked a brow and nodded. "Yeah, that's just what I said when they contacted me: 'what the fuck,' only it wasn't a question, just an okay. Now give me your wrist."

Still stunned, I raised my hand without question. He waved a small pen over my new tac, one issued to me just before we had dropped onto Exeter. The status lights faded, as did my skin. I noticed that his tac had also been deactivated, which was a violation of standing orders and punishable by imprisonment. We were out of contact with the Corps, and it would be very difficult to trace us. "What a minute—"

"C'mon. They're waiting."

"Who?"

"Who do you think? Come on."

"Activate my tac. Right now."

"Are you kidding?"

"I got a whole platoon here."

He smirked. "This place is crawling with Marines. They'll be busy. Trust me. And I'm sure that asshole Kohrana won't miss you. They'll report you MIA, just like me."

"What's going on?"

A round of particle fire ricocheted just outside the tunnel, followed by the low rumble of falling rock.

Halitov widened his gaze on the tunnel entrance. "No time for a heads up. Just follow me. You'll be glad you did." He started off, hunkering down as the ceiling closed in.

I didn't move. "So you're AWOL—is that what you're telling me?"

"Yup. And now so are you."

"What the hell are you doing here?"

He stopped, turned back. "Geez, I thought you'd be glad to see me. No, 'Rooslin, you're alive!' or 'Rooslin, you don't how much I've missed you. You're like a brother to me.' Shit."

"Will you tell me what's going on?"

Another round boomed outside.

"Goddamn it, Scott, come on! I found Paul. Actually, he found me, but who cares. Come on!"

And that set my boots in motion. "You found him? What about Dina?"

"You want to know about her? Then move your ass!"

Both of us tapped into the bond and maneuvered swiftly through the narrow tunnel, reached an oval-shaped cavern dimly lit by Halitov's light stick. He directed me toward a pool of calm water, about twenty meters across.

"Is she alive?"

"Just get in the water."

I grabbed his damp collar. "Fuck, man, you tell me right now. Is she alive?"

"Let him explain it to you."

"Who? Paul?"

"Just get in the water."

"Why all the secrecy?"

"Just get in the water!"

I splashed in and swore. "Jesus, it's ice!"

"You want a hot tub? Go to Club Io. Now listen to me. Swim straight out to the middle, then dive. Go down a couple meters. Feel your way to another tunnel. Go in. It turns right, then comes back up. You'll need the bond, or you won't make it."

After taking several deep breaths and reassuring myself that the bond was, in fact, tingling within me, I dived and followed his instructions, shivering as much from the cold water as from the thought that Dina might still be alive. The tunnel grew so narrow that I barely fit through, began to feel claustrophobic, panicked, kicked even harder, pushed myself up even faster, then, nearly out of breath, bleeding every ounce from my muscles but unable to will myself to the destination because I didn't know where we were going, my head cleared the surface. I took in a huge breath, blinked hard, saw lights flashing near me, heard voices, felt hands reach under my arms and begin dragging me toward the shore.

There, I looked up at the person who had set me down, but a light stick blinded me. I shielded my eyes from the glare.

"Sorry," came a familiar voice.

The light stick came down, revealing Lieutenant Paul Beauregard, son of Colonel J.D. Beauregard of the Colonial Wardens, once boyfriend of Dina and colleague of mine at the academy. He leaned over me, his now-bearded face tight with concern. Other than that beard and his long, ragged hair, he looked no worse for wear. Surprisingly, he had not aged like Rooslin and I had, with no crow's-feet near his eyes or gray at his temples.

"Paul," I said, still out of breath. "You made it."

His tone grew solemn. "I guess you could say that." He hunkered down, proffered his hand. "Come on. We'll get you dried off."

Behind him stood six or seven other guardsmen, their utilities ripped and dust-covered, with two sporting black bandanas. One, a pale redheaded guy who glanced suspiciously at me, turned away, splashed into the water, and helped Halitov to the shore.

"Who are they?" I asked Paul.

"We've set up a little camp. I'll tell you everything when we get there."

"And Dina?"

"Come on."

With a deep sigh over the continued secrecy, I took his hand, and he helped me up. Shivering and seeing my breath, I welcomed the blanket someone threw over me. We started along the shore, heading toward the entrance of a deep tunnel about a dozen meters ahead.

Rooslin jogged up next to me, clutching his own blanket and trembling. "He made it. You fuckin' believe that? He hijacks our ride, slips in past their defenses, and gets all the way here. That's courage, man. I knew we should've went with him. I knew it." I just shook my head as he added, "And have you seen his face? No accelerated aging. Nothing. Must be these caves."

"We'll see."

Paul led us through the tunnel, which forked into three more tunnels. We took the center shaft and walked for another ten minutes until Paul shouted, "Caveman!"

A voice came from the distance. "Caveman, acknowledged. All clear."

I realized he had just checked in with one of his perimeter guards so that we could pass. Very efficient. We moved under that guard, a dirty-faced guy no more than twenty who lay across an outcropping of stone some five meters above. As we turned a corner, sunlight poured into a wide chamber ahead, and the promise of warmth drove me past everyone else and alongside Paul.

"We found this place a few weeks ago. Moved our camp here," he explained, as we reached a gallery whose curving walls raced up perhaps one hundred meters to a natural skylight at least fifty meters in diameter. We were ants rummaging about the bottom of some enormous, dried-up well with a massive fissure wandering through its center. "Watch your step," he said, as we walked parallel to the fissure. "We've thrown rocks down there. They just drop away. No bottom. Or so it seems."

He led me across the chamber to their camp, a rather standard-looking military bivouac. Sleeping gear lay strewn about, along with several cargo containers bearing Western Alliance insignia. Several battery-powered portable heaters stood nearby, their tubes extending a full meter and glowing brilliantly.

I took a seat on the floor next to one of those heaters. "I was going to ask how you've been managing down here," I said, still examining the camp as he found a duffel, removed several towels, and tossed them to me. "Looks like you've been doing a little hit, grab, and run."

He crossed to one of the containers, removed a loaf

of real bread, tore it in half, and handed me a piece. "They keep sending Marines in here. We take out as many as we can, then we take their supplies. It's not genius work. Just survival." He handed the rest of the loaf to Halitov, who sat near me, took a barbaric bite, then stole one of my towels.

Paul's crew gathered around us, though I suspected he had left the sentries in place. Those with us didn't seem too pleased by my visit. One of them, the redhead who had pulled Halitov from the water, actually glowered at me.

Noticing this, Paul said, "Scott, this is Tommy McFarland. He and most of the others here were second years when the academy got attacked. They didn't get out like we did. They've been hiding here ever since, living off what they could steal and waiting for the counterattack."

I nodded to McFarland, whose glower did not soften, then I turned to Paul. "I do something to piss him off?"

"We know what you're going to do," said McFarland. "And we ain't going to let you do it. Without Paul, most of would be dead. We owe him our lives."

"What're you talking about?"

"I went AWOL," said Paul. "Of course, now we're all hoping to get out of here, but they know that when we do, you're going to turn me in. I'll be court-martialed, imprisoned, maybe even brainwiped. I don't think my father can help."

"Maybe he can."

He shrugged. "Point is, I know you, Scott. Always the code. You'll do the right thing. Turn me in."

"Excuse me, but last time I looked, there were Marines everywhere," began Halitov, still chomping on his bread. "We're debating what's going to happen after we escape. Let's worry about getting out of here first."

"Why don't we start from the beginning," I said, eyeing Halitov. "What happened to you?"

"Not his fault," Paul said. "We scored some short-range communications and monitored your drop here. When I found out you and Halitov were actually leading a company, I thought either the universe or Ms. Brooks was responsible, probably the latter. So I contacted Halitov, let him know where we were, told him I could deactivate his tac. We set up a meeting."

"Why didn't you contact me?" I asked. "I would've come."

"Like I said, Scott, I know you. I asked you to go AWOL when I wanted to take Dina here. You wouldn't come. I seem to remember your knife at my throat. So why would I expect you to go AWOL now? If anything, I figured you'd tell your CO that I was here in the caves so you could get permission to come and arrest me." Paul turned a mild grin on Halitov. "But he wanted to come the first time."

Thankfully, Halitov just nodded and didn't try talking with a huge chunk of bread in his mouth.

"So you thought he'd help you escape, only you didn't expect me to lead a special op in here," I concluded.

"That would be Ms. Brooks trying to help again. And you're right. I didn't expect you here, in the caves."

"So if I'm a threat to you, which explains all the looks your people are giving me"—I glanced to Mc-Farland—"then why'd you bring me here?"

Halitov backhanded bread crumbs from his lips, then wriggled his brows at me. "That's where I come in. I told him I wouldn't help unless it was you and I, together. I remember what you told Breckinridge. Figured I owed you."

"Thanks," I said with mock enthusiasm. "We can break the code together, become just like Breckinridge. Lie, cheat, steal, screw over our families . . ."

"Shut up with the fucking code," Halitov snapped. "There's so much dissension now, maybe there ain't no code anymore."

I grew deadly serious: "There is."

Halitov threw up his hands. "I don't get you. Why's the code so important?"

"It just is."

"No, that's not good enough. I've listened to that for too long. And don't give me that shit about being loyal." He marched up close and leaned into my face. "Well?"

I spun away. "My mother left when I was three. Know why? 'Cause of this." I whirled back and pointed to the birthmark on my cheek. "She couldn't hack a commitment to a kid like me. When the going got tough, she bailed. And you know, every time someone asks me why I'm so loyal to the code, I think about her, about what she did, and I know now I'll never turn my back on my family—and that family is the Corps."

"Look, we don't have time for this," interjected Paul, then he raised an index finger at me. "Your platoon is pushing back the Marines. We've been getting pretty good at tracking them, predicting their movements, but now they're on the run, and it's not safe anymore. We have to move out within the hour. What I'll need from you is a tawt-capable transport, preferably something small, like an ATC."

I couldn't stifle my chuckle. "You're crazy if you think I can get you one. And you're even more crazy if you think I'm going to let you leave without telling me what happened to Dina."

He nodded. "It's easier if I show you."

5 **⊙**   **As Paul, his** crew, Halitov, and I were about to
              depart the camp to see what had happened
to Dina, Paul handed me a bandana. "Blindfold. Put
it on."

"Why?" I asked.

"You trust me, I show you. You don't, you get
nothing."

"I don't understand."

"I don't care."

I looked to Halitov, who had already donned his
own blindfold. "Scott, just put the damned thing on,
will you?"

I hardened my gaze on Paul. "Too many secrets."

"And too little time."

Swearing under my breath, I tied the bandana
around my eyes. Paul checked to make sure the fabric
fit snugly around my eyes, then he grabbed my wrist
and we began a trek that lasted nearly an hour, with
me stumbling all the way.

I thought it painful how in all that darkness I found
it hard to summon up a clear picture of Dina's face. I
wondered if that inability said something about my
feelings for her. Did my heart ache from love, or guilt?
I wasn't sure.

"Okay," said Paul. "Take off your blindfold. Let
your eyes adjust."

I complied, and brownish gray walls undulated

around me until I realized that I was inside a tall, cylindrical chamber whose ceiling tapered up into a cone. The walls were not brown or gray or made of stone but comprised of some burnished alloy. I chanced another glance to that ceiling, saw just how vast the place was, and with a tingling sense of familiarity that finally warmed into full-on recognition, I realized where we were. "The pit with the catwalk around it and the big missilelike structure down below. We're inside that missile, aren't we?" I asked Paul.

"That's right. But it's no missile. And you'll never find your way back in here without me." He tipped his head to the opposite end of the cylinder, where, from behind a long bank of electronic equipment with octagonal displays, I caught sight of Dina. And gasped.

"Oh my God," was all Halitov could say.

"What is this?" I asked, barely able to look at her.

She hung above us, a frail, unconscious, naked woman attached to a gelatinous disk by thousands of hair-thin gossamers that reminded me of the tiny tubes inside the conditioning machines. If she was alive, there was no clear indication. She looked like an anorexic puppet crucified against a throbbing, pulsating drape of green and orange and black. Remarkably, the slash across her throat was fully healed, with no evidence of a scar. I suspected that the stab wound to her back was also gone, along with any signs of her decompression.

"Is she alive?" I asked.

"Barely," Paul replied, his eyes glassing up as he stared at her. "For the past few days her pulse has been growing weaker."

"But her wounds are gone," I said, gazing upon the

miracle as though it were a dream. "How did you know to get her here, to this place? What is it? A Racinian hospital or something?"

"I didn't bring her here. When I landed outside, Marines were right on my tail. I took a couple of rounds, got Dina near the catwalk. And that's the last thing I remember. I must've passed out. I woke up in here. My wounds were healed, and I found Dina up there."

"Someone must've helped you," I said.

"I don't know, but Dina's been here ever since." He spun to the bank of electronics. "I think there's a problem with this equipment. Until you guys arrived Alliance scientists over at the conditioning facility were trying to get the place back on-line. I think their experiments affected this place. I've tried gaining access, but even knowing the language doesn't help. Could be codes or DNA or something." He closed his eyes, rubbed the bridge of his nose. "We've turned these caves upside down looking for an answer. I still think maybe it's not the caves that have healing properties—it's this equipment. Maybe this whole place is emitting a fluctuation in the space-time continuum that allows it to reorganize the particles of your body to heal you."

"Look at us, Paul," I said. "Me and Halitov. We're getting old."

"I didn't want to say anything."

"You went through the same conditioning. You should be aging like us. You're not."

"Which supports my theory. But maybe the effect is only temporary. Maybe if I leave, the rapid aging will begin."

I gave a long, weary sigh. "Burning twice as bright . . . it's no fun at all."

"How long you think she's going to be up there?" asked Halitov.

Paul frowned. "Who knows. I thought about cutting her down, but I'm afraid that might kill her. These machines, they brought her back to life. But now . . . it's like she's dying on me all over again." With that, he slammed a fist on one of the alien panels. "Fuck!"

My gaze swept the room. "There has to be something we can do."

He stared gravely at me.

"I say we leave her up there," said Halitov. "Maybe her pulse is getting weaker 'cause it's supposed to. Maybe that's how the machine works. Just leave her up there until the machine releases her."

"Or till someone comes and takes her down," I said.

"Who?" asked Halitov. "One of the Racinians? Some old alien who's the guardian of this facility?"

"Maybe."

He made a silly face. "Fuckin' fantasyland you're living in. Probably some Racinian drone or something scooped them up, brought them here, hooked Dina up to the machine. Now a drone I can believe. We've already found evidence of drones in their ruins. At least all that history they dumped in my brain says so. Best thing is to leave her. See what happens."

"You mean we wait here in the caves?" I asked. "For how long?"

"As long as it takes," answered Paul, shifting to get in my face. "But not we. Me. You'll lead my people out, but I'm not leaving her."

A cadet named Hollis, a hard-faced woman with dark hair pulled back in a ponytail, came forward. "Sir, with all due respect, sir. I speak for the others when I say that if you stay, we stay. Sir."

As much as I disagreed with Paul's decision to go AWOL to try to save Dina's life, I admired his loyalty to her and the loyalty he inspired in his crew. You could see it burning in Hollis's eyes. She would give her life for Paul in a heartbeat, and that was just the kind of fierce dedication I needed from my own people.

Paul's tone grew sympathetic as he gripped Hollis's shoulder. "When we get back to camp, you're all getting out with these guys."

"No, sir."

"C'mon. All you ever talk about is getting out of here. What about that slice of New York pizza you said you were going to buy? What about your parents? You don't think they're waiting for you? You don't think the brass'll issue you a leave so you can see them? Your entire life has been put on hold. You've been living in a cave, for God's sake."

"But sir—"

"No. I won't have it. I owe you a ticket out. And you're getting one. End of discussion."

Paul's little speech doused the fire in Hollis's eyes. She swung away, dejected. "Yes, sir."

I cleared my throat. "Of course, I can't allow you to stay," I told Paul.

"Of course."

"So where does that leave us?"

He cocked a brow. "At war, I'd say."

I closed my eyes, stiffened. "Paul, I have to do my job."

"Your job," he began darkly, then shouted, "Look at her! Open your eyes and look at her! People are what's important—not duty, not honor, not the Corps. My father was wrong. Everything they told us at the academy is wrong. It's all bullshit. In the end, we're all we got."

After glancing painfully at Dina, I narrowed my gaze on him. "What if she doesn't love you?"

"You asked me that once before. And my answer's still the same: I know she doesn't love me. But I don't care."

"You're a fool," said Halitov.

Nearly in unison, Paul and I told him, "Shut up!"

"I was going to say you both are fools," Halitov said. "Scott, if Paul wants to stay, let him stay. We take the rest out. We don't have to lie. We just don't volunteer the fact that we ran into him. That's all."

"And that's all I'm asking," said Paul.

"See?" said Halitov. "One big happy family again."

I glanced at Halitov, then at Paul, wondering whether I should keep the secret because I understood how Paul felt about Dina, understood it as intimately as anyone could.

Then, fortunately, I realized I didn't need to make that decision. "Paul, if I leave you here with her, I'm signing your death tag. There's an Alliance fleet up there. Chances are high they're going to drop a major ground force here and take back this moon. That happens, the only way you'll get off this rock is as a POW. And since you're conditioned, I'm betting they'll brainwipe you and put you back out there, fighting for the wrong side. We have to get out. Now."

"I'll take my chances. But you're right. You do need to leave. Blindfolds on. Let's go."

"Fuck the blindfold," said Halitov. "If you can't trust us now . . ."

"I got very little to bargain with," he said. "The way in here stays with me."

I looked at Paul, saw that for the time being there would be no more arguing with him. I figured that once we returned to camp, I'd try one last time to convince him. If he did not comply, then I knew, God, I knew, what I had to do.

I didn't plan on passing out, just five minutes into our trek back. A wave of dizziness hit, a tingling rose through my spine, and I swore as I surrendered to the inevitable.

"Holy shit. Scott, wake up."

There are many faces I can appreciate after a stretch of unconsciousness—but Rooslin Halitov's isn't one of them. He gaped at me, all big jowls and pointy jaw.

"I'm awake," I said. "What's going on? We blacked out, didn't we?" My gaze focused, and I got a better look at him. "Holy shit is right."

Halitov appeared as fresh and young as the first day I had met him at the academy. No gray. No wrinkles.

"Fuckin' fountain of youth, man," he cried.

"No," said Paul, now hovering over us. "If I'm right, that machine is just correcting a problem. Like you said, when you leave, the aging might return."

"Then it's just a damned tease," Halitov said, bolting to his feet. "Damn! But then again, maybe it isn't!"

I glanced up, saw the stars peeking through a twilit sky, and got my bearings. We were back in Paul's camp. "What time is it?"

"About twenty-one hundred local," said Halitov.

"Twenty-one hundred? Damn, we have to get out of here." I sat up, touched my eyes, which didn't feel very different, the skin near them perhaps a bit smoother.

"Want to look?" asked Paul, tossing me a standard-issue pocket mirror. Sure enough, my own gray and wrinkles were gone. I even felt more agile. "You got thirty more seconds to admire yourself," he continued. "Then I'm reactivating your tacs, and you're taking my people out."

"Okay."

He did a double take. "Okay?"

"Yeah. I'm going to leave you here. With her."

"You're bluffing."

"I'm not." I rose, faced him squarely. "You know, Jarrett used to talk a lot like you. He never believed in any of the things I believe in. He never wanted to be a soldier. But you . . . you've always struck me as hard-core."

"Yeah, when your father's commanding the Colonial Wardens, everybody thinks you're going to follow in Dad's footsteps. I've always hated not having a choice."

"Guess I'd feel the same."

Perhaps my lingering bitterness over my brother's death—or supposed death—made me strike back at the Corps by doing something I swore I'd never do: let Paul stay. Or maybe I just felt sorry for him, for a life dictated by his father's choices, not his own. To this day, I'm still uncertain what really made me change my mind, but the act would later have an interesting and unexpected effect on Paul.

"All right, people," Paul called in a familiar command tone. "Take them up through tunnel eight."

McFarland and two others nodded, as Paul waved his little magic wand over my tac, reactivating it. He did likewise to Halitov. I immediately skinned up and called upon my tactical computer to show me the whereabouts of my platoon.

The image of two ATCs already airborne robbed my breath. The entire platoon had already evacuated the caves. "Kohrana, copy?"

"Is that you, St. Andrew?"

"Affirmative."

"Thought we lost you, just like your XO."

"Negative. Tac malfunction. And I've located my XO and about a dozen cadets who've been hiding here since the first attack."

"Get up to the main entrance. We're coming back for you."

"Negative. What's the status on that Alliance fleet?"

"Troop carriers en route. They'll make moonfall in approximately twenty-one minutes."

I ordered my computer to pull up a satellite image of those carriers. My God, there must have been a thousand of them, each jetting a full platoon toward the academy grounds.

"Just get back," I told Kohrana. "I know another way out of here. And do me a favor: relay my status to Disque. Ask him to hold back one ATC for us. Have it wait out in the canyon below Whore Face."

"Aye-aye. And hey, St. Andrew. You're an asshole . . . but good luck."

"Yeah," I said with a snort. "Thanks."

I de-skinned, glanced around at Paul's ragtag

team. "There's a tunnel that'll take us all the way back to the academy, out near Whore Face."

"They know it," said Paul. "But from here it'll take at least an hour to get there. I'll contact the pilot for you, tell him to hang low until you're almost there."

"Thanks." I regarded the group. "All right. Let's gear up and go." Abruptly realizing that I might never see the colonel's son again, I offered my hand. "Come with us."

He took the hand, shook firmly. "If she does wake up, I don't want her in there alone. I have enough supplies to last a couple more months. They won't find me in there."

"I hope you're right." I turned, accepted a particle rifle from McFarland, then started off.

"Scott?" Paul called after me. I glanced back. "If you ever run into my father, don't tell him what happened here. Don't tell him anything."

I nodded and almost wished I had shared with him how the Wardens wanted to recruit me as part of their plan to push the new colonial government in the right direction. But telling him that his father was organizing a "mild" coup would only deepen his disillusionment.

We moved as quickly and stealthily as we could, though Halitov and I could have accessed the bond and traversed the passageways in seconds instead of minutes. McFarland assumed command of the cadets, and while he wasn't thrilled about still answering to me, he behaved professionally and even thanked me for allowing Paul to remain behind. Five minutes into our trek, we reached an intersection, where a much wider tunnel cut at a forty-five-degree angle across our path, and smack in the middle of it lay a hole with a diameter of about two meters, with an identical one bored into the ceiling. "What do we got?" I asked McFarland, as we paused and hunkered down near the wall.

"The machines below us emit some kind of a pulse wave, which comes up through here. I wouldn't get too close to that hole. There . . . there's one now."

The ground rumbled for a moment before a shimmering blue-green orb shot up from the floor and passed through the hole in the ceiling. Two seconds later, another one came. Two more seconds, and the third rocketed skyward. They kept coming at two-second intervals.

"I've seen this before," I said, remembering the night Dina and I had jogged out to the canyon. We had been getting ready to leave when she had spotted the light show in the distance. Now I stood directly over the source.

"We've thrown rocks at them," said McFarland. "And they get vaporized."

"You got point," I told him. "Let's move."

He rose and dashed off, with Halitov just behind him. I waved on the others, then pulled up the rear. I neared the pit and paused as the orbs shot past me. A strange compulsion to touch one drew me toward the hole, my arm extended, fingers twitching as they neared the eerily beautiful light. Just a few inches away. One inch. A hairsbreadth.

Suddenly, the quantum bond surged within me. At the beginning of the universe, all matter was one. All time was one. Time and space have expanded, but at that moment I found myself watching nebulae coalesce into stars and black holes grow bright as they returned to their original states. Billions of galaxies gathered toward a central region as I surveyed it all from a spectacular vantage point. McFarland, I realized, had been wrong about the rocks. They were not vaporized but transported to another space, another time.

Over the years I've shared the experience with close friends, but I'm often told that it was either my imagination or, perhaps, an image put in my head by the machines. In any event, the vision seemed to confirm what we suspect about the origin of the universe and how the mnemosyne allow us to tap into that most basic, most powerful of forces. I've come to theorize that the emissions are not created by the machine but represent a natural seam in the fabric of the space-time continuum. The ancient Racinians located this seam running through Exeter and opted to build their conditioning facility and machines close to it, perhaps in an attempt to harness its power.

And what power I sensed, though the entire experience lasted no more than a few seconds. Multiple rounds of particle fire jarred me away from the orbs and toward the tunnel ahead, where Paul's people were shouting.

More gleaming rounds split the air just a quarter meter left of my head as I reached the rearmost cadet, a scrawny woman whose name I had already forgotten. She had skinned up but had kept the shield near her face clear. She looked scared. "McFarland says we got two snipers up ahead."

"And I say we got no time for this." I found the

bond, skinned up, and bolted past the line of cadets, running directly into the snipers' fire.

Either McFarland or Halitov called me, I wasn't sure. My name echoed through the tunnel as the snipers' beads narrowed and struck my abdomen for all of two seconds before I willed them away, bending them back toward their sources.

I saw the first sniper to my left. He had scaled a stalagmite and had roped himself tightly to it, up near the tunnel's roof. His own stream of fire burrowed into his combat skin, weakened it, broke through, then tore apart his chest—before he knew what had happened. I didn't spot the second sniper until I heard the death groan, off to the right. I jogged a few meters farther, saw him scrunched into a shallow depression in the cave wall, near the floor.

Rooslin came running over, raised his brow at the dead Marine. "I still have trouble doing that. One of these days you're going to teach me."

I sighed and scanned our course. "All clear. Move out."

Once again, I pulled up the rear, and occasionally I'd look up to see my brother leading the way, with Dina and Clarion just behind him. I'd shiver off the déjà vu and the memories and warily keep moving.

No light poured into the tunnel to indicate we neared its end, but we had been traveling for nearly an hour. McFarland called for a halt. I double-timed up the line and joined him and Halitov as we dropped to our bellies and crawled outside, onto the bluff opposite Whore Face. We shifted past the wide lip of rock that concealed the tunnel entrance from the riverbed below. I skinned up and zoomed in on the canyon floor below Whore Face, not far from the spot where Cavalier had died.

"C'mon, Disque, you old prick. Don't let me down," I muttered as I panned the area, searching for the quad-winged silhouette of an ATC.

And wouldn't you know, an ATC came roaring over old Whore Face, turned on its starboard wings, and descended smartly toward the canyon floor.

"Paul must've gotten through to the pilot," said Halitov.

I scrolled through a communications data bar and locked onto the pilot's frequency. "ATC Delta Five-Six, copy?"

"Copy, Captain. Ready to load and dust off in one mike, copy?"

"Copy. We'll be there."

"Better move, Captain. We got troop carriers dropping all over the place."

"I hear that. Stand by."

Two things happened at once. Actually, three things, though the latter was less alarming.

Even as the ATC's skids touched ground, an artillery nest on our side of the riverbed opened up on the ship, launching heavy particle rounds that struck and began weakening the vessel's combat skin.

Behind us, back in the tunnel, that familiar and dreaded sound of rifle fire returned, along with a scream: "I'm hit! Oh my God! I'm hit! I'm hit!" Paul's people began pouring out of the tunnel, with a few trailing behind, shifting backward and firing wildly into the darkness.

I traded a look with Halitov, realizing with a start that he was returning to his aged self right before my eyes. I opened my mouth, about to mention it as I sprang to my feet and brought my rifle to bear.

An explosion below stole my attention.

The ATC had been trying to climb away from the mortar fire when its shield had finally succumbed. Our ride out burst into dozens of fire-licked fragments that lit up the canyon wall as they plummeted toward the riverbed.

I whirled away from the destruction, even as an Alliance Marine darted from the tunnel, took a half dozen rounds from Paul's people, then fell—but not before spraying the area with a wild bead. I craned my head, even as McFarland, who was just skinning up, took a round just above his Adam's apple. Direct spine shot. No chance of resuscitation.

"There's a whole squad in there," cried the scrawny woman I had been following. "Here they come!"

"Fuck. What do we now?" Halitov asked darkly.

I gave him a funny look. Wasn't it obvious? "Run!"

6 ▶ **I waved on** Paul's group, ordering them to take the rocky path down toward the riverbed, where our ATC lay burning and strewn across the dust. Halitov took point, which he wasn't thrilled about, but he and I were the only conditioned officers, and I planned on stalling those Marines still inside the tunnel.

We had already lost McFarland and two other cadets, but the rest made it out and charged in behind Halitov. As the scrawny woman passed me, she asked, "What do we do now, sir, with no ride home?"

"Not your problem. You worry about dropping more Marines and clearing our path."

"Aye-aye, sir!"

For a nanosecond, I wished her problems were mine. I was the one who had to find us another ride, and as my gaze lifted skyward, all I saw were the running lights of Western Alliance crab carriers and smaller troop carriers descending like multicolored meteors in slow motion. Antiaircraft guns operated by tactical computers, their human operators already aboard escape shuttles, sent streaming globules of white-hot fire toward those colorful lights.

Crouching tightly against the lip of rock, I braced myself, planning on using the bond and the quitunutul arts to launch myself at the first Marine to exit. With the *gozt* I'd take him out, even as I aimed my rifle at the next soldier. The maneuver and its result shone so vividly in my mind's eye that when I caught my first glimpse of the Marine, his combat skin fluctuating from black to a dusty brown, I gave little thought to the fact that my conditioning might fail me. I saw what I needed to do. Waited. Spotted him.

I sprang from the rock, launched myself into the air, and felt nothing but a meager rebound from the bluff. I rose a couple of meters and would have made a respectable *gozt* into the Marine's chest, had he not easily dodged my advance and opened fire.

Two more Marines joined the first, adding twin thunderclaps of fire that riddled my combat skin with rounds and set alarms flashing in my HUV. The tactical computer reported evenly, "Skin at forty percent and falling. Estimated penetration in nine seconds. Eight, seven, six—"

I tried rolling out of their beads.

"Five, four, three—"

Tried to reach the path, where the nearest boulder shaped like a blunt arrowhead stood, offering good cover.

"Two, one—"

My last word was nothing profound, just a simple recognition of the inevitable: "Shit."

A slight sting rushed through my shoulder as I came out of the roll, bumped my head on the boulder, then saw the three Marines drop, all shot in the back by someone inside the tunnel. A skinned figure charged out, his shield glistening a moment before trickling away.

Even as I stared at my rescuer, data bars flashed, reporting that my shoulder wound was only superficial and being attended to by the suit.

"You all right?" Paul asked, lowering his rifle, his cheeks red and tear-stained. He grabbed my wrist, yanked me to my feet.

"You coming with us?"

"Yeah. It was like she knew," he gasped.

"What're you talking about? Who knew?"

"Dina."

"What happened?"

"She's gone, Scott. I went back to check on her, and I thought I heard her in my mind. She told me it was all right. She told me to go. Then the machine just . . . stopped. I checked her pulse. She's gone." He choked up once more. "I guess even the Racinians can't raise the dead."

I nodded. "I'm sorry, Paul."

He wiped off a tear. "I tried to get her down from the machine. I couldn't detach those tubes, those things. We'll come back for her body. I swear. Let's get the hell out of here."

We hightailed it down the path, exploiting the boulders for cover and catching up with the rest of the group within a few minutes. Halitov and the others were as surprised as I was by Paul's appearance. Whispering, I told Halitov of Dina's death, and he nodded and went to Paul.

"I'm sorry," Halitov told the colonel's son.

"Let's get to that talus and scree near the base. It'll make good cover," Paul said quickly, burying his pain in the business of escape. He craned his head toward me. "If that's okay with you?"

Had he uttered his last sentence with sarcasm, I would've returned the same, but he had said that in earnest, remembering that I was senior officer. "You're used to being in charge. Don't let me stop you—and you're still in command of these people. Just answer to me."

"Thanks."

Down below, hidden behind cracked shoulders of stone that had dropped off the hillside, we stared gravely at the dying embers of our ATC.

"Situation assessment," said Halitov, glancing around for effect. "Multiple enemy carriers dropping hundreds of troops. Friendlies have already evacked. No chance of another ATC getting through their defenses and said troops dispersing to terminate remaining enemy personnel—meaning us. Short version: we're fucked."

"That's correct, Mr. Halitov," said Paul in a tone so formal that it reminded me of our academy days. "And they're hitting the jackpot, taking three conditioned officers into custody."

"That can't happen," I said.

Paul nodded. "We'll kill ourselves first."

"Fuck that," cried Halitov. "You want to join your girlfriend, go ahead. We're not following."

"Hey, *Captain*," I said, reminding the whiner of his rank. "Have you looked in the mirror? You're dying anyway."

"And not alone. But I'll take whatever time I got left. I want to get back. Get a couple of hookers and go on a two-week R&R. I want to die while getting laid. And I want Breckinridge to watch, so she can see what she could've had."

"Wait a minute," I said. "Maybe we have an ace in the hole—if she's still talking to me." I ordered my tac to show me classified comm channels and found the one Kristi Breckinridge had used to contact me. Time for a long-distance call with the minutes billable to the Seventeen System Guard Corps.

The link established, despite the enemy's jamming the standard battle frequencies, and the time delay was reduced significantly by new communications technology inspired by the Racinians and having something to do with rerouting the signal through a space-time fluctuation field. At that moment, I could have cared less about the physics.

"St. Andrew. It's about time," she said, her voice cracking ever so slightly. "I've been monitoring your progress."

"Our ATC got tommyed."

"I know."

"Can we bum a ride?"

"That's pretty glib for a man who's surrounded by over ten thousand enemy troops."

"Forget the details. Concentrate on this: I found Halitov. And Paul. They're both safe and with me."

"What about Dina Forrest?"

"She's dead."

"All right, then. The rest of the fleet's getting ready to tawt out, but one of our endo/exo skimmers has just tawted in to cover the retreat. I'll contact the colonel and have that ship punch a hole in the Alliance's artillery and send down a dropshuttle for you."

"Were it that easy. ETA?"

"Give me about twenty minutes."

"Uploading coordinates now."

"Receiving. Just stay alive."

"Oh, we will. Just don't leave us here. Understand?" I broke the link before she could reply and shared the news with Halitov and Paul.

"Now we're really in bed with her," said Halitov.

"What are you bitching about?" I asked. "Isn't that what you want?"

He rolled his eyes, checked the charge on his rifle.

"Those skimmers are pretty awesome," said Paul. "Lightest, fastest ships in the fleet. Our taxi blew up, so they're sending down a limo. Not bad. That Breckinridge sounds like a player."

"Yeah, she's a player, all right. And she works for your father."

Paul sobered and shifted off, spying the riverbed.

"Well, all we have to do is wait," said Halitov. "And not get—"

Particle fire boomed over his words and sheared off gaping pieces of rock. We ducked behind a long slab of stone, about bench height, and I crawled toward its edge, even as the incoming continued. Peering around the edge, I zoomed in on our attackers: a squadron of Marines lying on their bellies and strung out along the top of Whore Face.

Fire punched gaping holes in the ground just a meter from my boots, and our cover began crumbling before our eyes. I crawled back to Halitov and Paul and reported the squadron.

"They know if they keep firing, we won't stay here," Paul said.

"I'm surprised they haven't used any A-three," said Halitov.

Paul and I put our index fingers to our lips. The big